SPECTOR

BASED ON A TRUE STORY

Elvis Slaughter

CONTENTS

"WRITTEN IN A conversational tone, *Spector*, is a must-read memoir for anyone having to steer through the healthcare system and a wakeup call for healthcare service providers. Spector is based on a true story." Elvis Slaughter

CHAPTER ONE

Washington Home
Mississippi, 1960

IN THE DISTANCE, thunder rumbled. A young boy responsively looked up, whipping his head toward the sky as an active retort. As far as he could see, bright sparks of lightning had muted the hot ambiance of the sun. He stole a glance at his mother from the yard; she, already done toiling in the fields for the day, had begun making night repasts for the family. A grumble from his tummy reminded the famished boy to be grateful she had begun to cook dinner. Soon, she would call for him to come inside. His gaze and attention returned to the bunch of sticks before him, which he used to construct a tiny house for play. Inside the house, four rocks represented the people living inside: the most massive rock belonged to Papa; the one next to it, slightly smaller, represented Mama; and the final two little stones were he and his sister. He continued whiling away the time in his imaginary world while sitting among stalks of grass.

"Will!"

He shifted his gaze from his stones to the source of the sound, a young girl with a smile beaming upon her face.

"What is it, Bethany?" He was hungry and irritated, which made him want to hear what she had to say even less.

"You wanna play a game?" she asked.

"Nah," he answered, feeling that whatever she had planned couldn't be more intriguing than his make-believe world, a world in which he could decide everything. Bethany scurried toward him with her hands cupped together. She put forth her conjoined hands, moving them closer to Will's face. He was about to dismiss her attempt and move his head back until he noticed the bright green gleam piercing through the slits between Bethany's fingers.

"Awwwnnn. Why not?" She furrowed her brows for a moment as if demanding an answer. By now, Will was quite curious to know if it was what he suspected it was.

"I got something. Wanna see?" she asked eagerly, crouching to his level and opening the space between her fingers a little more so he could see clearly.

"Light bug!" William cried, dropping his sticks into the dirt without a second thought. "It's a light bug!"

"Light-ning bug," she corrected him. "Say it right. Light-ning-bug." Bethany retracted her hands, much to his dismay. "Say it right, and I'll let you hold it."William yanked himself up, teetering on his stumpy legs. Hands outspread, he sprung forward toward his sister.

"Lie-ning-bug! Gimme the lie-ning-bug!" Not realizing where he was headed, his toe caught on the stick house he had crafted minutes earlier and he stumbled, collapsing onto the earth. "Aaaaaaaaaaarrrgggghhhhhhh!" he shrieked. He kept groaning in pain while his sister checked up on his wound.

Lifting his face off the ground, Bethany could see tears and dirt jumbled all over his face. His shoulders quivered profusely, leading her to let go of her captive by mistake.

"It's okay, Will. Here, get up," she said, stooping down to him. "Come on, Will."

"Bethany! William!" A voice they were well familiar with beckoned from the house. They could see their mother, Angela Washington, standing in the doorway of their home.

"What you doin' out here? I know y'all ain't gettin' into trouble." She folded her arms, a scowl visible on her face, and looked straight at her elder child. Bethany was aiding Will in his attempt to get back into an ideal position.

"We're fine, Mama," called Bethany. William howled as his sister tugged him upward from underneath his arms. "I've got 'im. We're fine."

With an "O-kay!" from their mother and the snap of the door, the siblings were alone again. William's breathing was going back to normal, but the tears remained on his chubby cheeks.

"Here, Will, do you want a lightning bug? I'll catch you one," Bethany offered. William shook his head vigorously.

"What about your sticks? Do you want your sticks?"

"Those are MINE!" he bellowed, surprisingly loud given his age. All four years of his existence seemed to push that statement out of his jaws. "No! Mine!" He plopped himself in the dirt, firmly planting his body between his sister and the remnants of his stick house.

"Fine," Bethany said, clearly annoyed by her kid brother's tantrums. She had only tried to help! She turned on her heel and scampered off. She cupped her hands as she chased the glowing green insects around their home.

With his annoying sister now out of his way, William returned his focus to his stick house. Their mother had called, but he would set his stick house right before going to dinner. His fall had shaken the foundation of the house, rendering it lopsided. He restarted from scratch by swiping his hand through the center of his home and continued with his reconstruction. What had been a calm and tender breeze had become aggressive gusts of wind, flinging leaves, dust, and small rocks at William and his project. The light around him dimmed. Looking up, William could see thick clouds passing in front of the sun, sending him into sudden darkness. He turned his face to resume playing when a movement in the distance caught his attention.

He froze in place, looking at the spot where he saw it. Was it a man? Was it a horse? What if it was a monster, or what if it was this God that Mama and Daddy talked about? As he stared and willed the presence to reveal itself again, Bethany came charging toward him.

"I think it's gonna rain!" she cried. "We should go in, Will." She stooped down to grasp his hand, but he did not budge. "Come on, little Will. We need to go into the house."

William pointed in the direction where the thing had appeared. "What is that?" he asked.

"What's what?"

He extended his arm and shook it up and down. "I saw something!"

Bethany shook her head. "Then we need to go inside, Will," she pressed, yanking his other arm. "Come on, or I'll get Daddy out here."

"Fine then," he pouted. "I'm staying here to see it. I'm not scared." He kept his gaze fixed on the area while Bethany trotted away to the safety of the house.

As the door sprung to a close with a quick *ra-tat*, William started to have a feeling. The back of his head felt funny, or was that his neck? Come to think of it, both of them felt funny. He braced against the quickening pace of the wind. A low rumble in the distance signaled a coming storm that would dampen the fields and expose the cracks in the leaky roof of the Washington family's house. Although Bethany ducked for cover the second, she saw a storm coming, William was notoriously fearless in the face of thunderstorms, much to the chagrin of his mother. Knowing that Angela would likely be out soon to drag him to the safety of the house, William got to his feet to investigate the space where he had noticed the presence.

He reached the edge of the yard, where the grass faded into a dusty dirt path. He stopped here, looked around, and saw nothing as he had before. He pattered down the path away from home, and as he progressed farther away, the flora increased in size. Instead of modest shrubs and plants, he found himself surrounded by the woods that had stood here for generations before him. Here and there, one of Bethany's beloved lightning bugs illuminated the air, the magic glow contrasting sharply with the dull shadows cast by the storm clouds. A boom of thunder shattered the solitude of the scene and William stumbled backward. Deciding to turn back around and go home, he stopped and yelled.

"Hello?" he called. No response. "Hell-ooooooo?" he repeated, a little louder. Still nothing. He spread his feet wide, cupped his hands around his mouth, and howled. "HELL-OOOOOOOOOOOOO?"

Another thunderclap split the sky above him. As a drizzle fell, William trotted back in the direction of home. Unable to see a tree root sticking up in the path, his foot connected and he toppled forward, much as he had earlier when he was playing with his sister. He screamed, then looked up to find someone looking back at him.

"Hello?" he whispered, breathless from the fall. He was staring into the face of a dazzling bright phantom that emitted a white glow. It sat mounted atop a horse that was equally stunning in its brilliance.

"Little William," murmured the rider. "You should be careful out here in this weather."

"You know my name?" William asked. "Who are you? Are you God?"

The ghost grinned, his teeth gleaming in the light that emanated from him and his steed. "No, I am not God," he replied. "You can call me Spector. I suppose it is about time that we meet. Come; I will guide you home."

Spector grabbed the reins of his horse in his left hand and lifted his right, signaling for William to follow. The horse loped along at a gentle gait so that the young boy could keep up.

"How did you find me?" William yelled as he scampered along.

"I have been with you for a long time," Spector called, raising his voice to be audible over the rainfall. "Since the day you were born, I have watched you grow and kept you from harm. I had plans to show myself to you when you were older, but now, I find the need to do this sooner." Spector pulled the reins toward himself and stopped the horse. "Are you all right, William?"

The rain was coming down in sheets now. William's ragged clothes were sodden and his shoes squelched in the mud. "I just want to be home!" he cried.

"We're almost there. It's just a little way more. You can make it there," Spector encouraged, waving his hand. With this gesture, William's feet were able to cross the wet ground as if it were bone dry.

"Whoa," William said. "How did you do that!?"

Spector ignored the question. "So, back to the house, we go." He urged his horse forward again, taking care to let little William stay nearby.

"Where did you come from?" asked William, his insatiable childish curiosity becoming more evident with every question.

"I would say that I have been here for a long time. I live in the shadows, in the spaces where you would not look for someone or something. I have kept an eye on your mother and your sister, Bethany. You, William, have caught my attention more than they have, and I have noted your sensitivity to my presence. Perhaps you had not realized it before; I can accept that. As I said, it would have been my preference to have this meeting when you were older and more able to understand, but the circumstances are beyond my control. It had to be now."

"'Circumstances?'" William asked. "What is 'circumstances'?"

"See, this is what I mean," Spector continued. "I suppose you could say it is the way things are. Right now, our 'circumstances' are that we are outside in this pesky storm."

Spector raised his right arm and swiped it in a half-circle above his head. As he did so, the intensity of the raindrops lightened. The rumble of thunder was no longer booming, instead softly grumbling in the distance.

"Are you a witch?" demanded William. "Are you the devil? Mama warned me about him!"

Roaring with laughter, Spector shook his head. "I can assure you, dear boy, I am not the devil nor a witch! I told you, I am Spector. Think of me as your new friend. I am here because I have an important message I have to tell you before you go home tonight."

As they emerged from the trees, William noticed light coming out of the windows of his house. He was almost in the safety of his house, back with his mama, papa, and sister! He could go inside, eat supper, and fall asleep in just a few moments once he had scurried over the threshold!

"William, please wait." Spector paused at the edge of the path. "This is your last night here."

The boy was partway across the yard when the words fell on his ears. He stopped short and turned around to face Spector. "What? Am I leaving? Where am I going?" William howled as the news set in. "You're taking me away?"

"No, no, no, I'm not taking you anywhere! Here, let me come to you." Spector dismounted his horse and walked toward William, who had collapsed in a sobbing heap on the ground. The horse stayed in place and made no sign of leaving. To look him in the eyes, Spector squatted down to William's level. "Shhh, William, I mean you no harm. You have a bright future ahead. Your mother is taking you and Bethany to a new place tomorrow. It will be better for you later on; there's nothing for you here besides the fields."

"But I like it here!" William bawled. "I don't want to go away!"

"Listen to me," Spector pressed. "Your mama loves you and your sister very much. There is nothing she does better than look after you two. You will like Illinois. You'll have more to see and do, and you'll have school. Life will be better for you there."

The new word caught William off guard. "Illi—what? Illin…"

"Illinois," Spector coached. "Ill-in-oy. It's where Abraham Lincoln came from. You could be like Honest Abe himself." Spector paused to smile at William, but the sentiment did not carry much weight with the blubbering toddler. "Your mama wants you to go to a nice school and have things that she couldn't have here in Mississippi. It's going to be alright, Will." Spector reached out his ghostly right hand toward William. "I can promise you that. Do you want to shake on it?"

Hesitant to touch this figure, William did not return the gesture immediately. He examined the outstretched hand before he looked the man in the face. He was unlike anyone William had seen before; he didn't look like a black man, but he didn't look like one of the white men, either. His eyes were not large or round but narrow with sharp corners. His nose was large and hooked, and up close William could even see that the man had long hair. When the man did not take his hand back, William decided to try and touch him.

It was as if he had grabbed onto a lightning bolt itself! Energy coursed from the man's hand through William's tiny fingers and palm, radiating upward to his shoulder. The prickly sensations he had felt in his head and neck earlier came back with a vengeance, and this time, they were painful. Crying out in shock, William released his grip on Spector's hand and recoiled, then resumed crying.

"Oh my, William; I am so sorry!" Spector exclaimed. "I should have told you that it might tickle a little bit. You poor boy. First, you find out you're moving hundreds of miles away, and then you touch a spooky stranger who shocks you!" He laughed while William stared at him, hiccoughing and sniveling.

"As I was saying, you will be moving tomorrow. Your mama has already packed up the car. She will break the news to your father tomorrow, which will be for the best. I have been unable to travel far in my previous attempts, but I am going to try as hard as I can to follow you to your new destination so that I can guide you. I will be in communication with others like me to watch you in the meantime."

"Others?" William piped up. "Are you an angel?"

At this, Spector smiled. "Sure, you can call me an angel. I can be your guardian, and my other angels will keep you safe." A grin broke out across William's face for the first time since Spector had revealed himself. "But you have to do a few things for me. I need you to be good and do what your mother asks. I need you always to be curious and ask questions. Finally, when you see me or any other angels—"

He took a moment to let the word hang.

"—you will listen to everything we advise you to do. Do you understand, William?"

"Yes, sir," William said.

"Good! Now, I won't touch you again, but I can help you get back up." Spector stood upright, then turned his palm skyward and raised his hand. As if he were a puppet on a string, William felt himself rising upward until he was on his feet instead of his bottom.

"Are you sure you're not a witch?" William asked.

Spector laughed again. "I'm sure I'm not a witch. Now, you need to get home before your mother worries. I think I hear her now. Goodbye, for now, William." Turning around, Spector approached his steed, mounted, and rode off. William watched them leave, tempted to stay in that spot as if glued to it, but a familiar sound broke his reverie.

"William Isaiah Washington!" His mother was shouting to summon him back home. "Boy, you better get back to this house, I swear!"

"Mama!" Seeing his mother in the front door, William pivoted around and took off for the house. He was so happy to see her that he did not immediately register the anguish in her face. "I'm coming, Mama!" He reached the doorstep and darted inside past her.

"Who were you talking to out there?" she demanded. "Is there someone outside?"

"Just my friend, Spector," William confessed. "He's a good friend."

"Spector?" Angela squinted her eyes and jerked her head backward. "What is a Spector? Are you sick?"

"Nope!" He ran off to find Bethany so he could tell her everything that had just happened.

When her child was out of sight, Angela stepped outside into the darkness and looked around to see if anyone or anything was casing the house. Wildlife was a common culprit, but in this day and age, she was never too careful. There was no sign of anyone or anything; perhaps the "Spector" that her son had mentioned was just in his imagination. She took a deep breath of the autumn air before going back inside and locking the door. As Spector had predicted, it was the last night the Washington family would spend under the roof of their home in Mississippi.

CHAPTER TWO

North Suburban Hospital
Illinois, 1997

A s his mother lay on her hospital bed, William Washington took a moment to study his mother's intricate features. She looked calm and peaceful, her gray hair falling to the sides of her face. The crinkles at the corner of her eyes had been prominent for as long as he could remember, but the creases had deepened with time. His gaze guided him to the lower part of her face and he could see her thick lips preceding the firm chin, which he took after.

"God is good," Bethany enthused. "He has brought our mother through this difficulty and allowed us to keep her. God is so good." A pause ensued as if she was waiting on an affirmation from William but he, deep in his thoughts, remained silent.

"Wouldn't you say so?" she asked, prompting him to respond.

William considered his sister's words for a moment before making a guttural noise in response. "Ungh."

The beeping noises of the monitors punctuated his pause. William never liked the ominous sounds they made, but who does? A nurse came in to check on the patient.

"Good afternoon," she greeted them all, her voice light and airy. "I'm sorry to interrupt, but may I check a few things for Ms. Washington?" she asked politely while gesturing to their mother, who was resting peacefully on the bed. William gave his approval.

"I'm going to go get a coffee from the cafeteria," Bethany said as she stood up. She knew neither of them had left their mother's side in hours and felt they both needed a break; William, especially. "Will, you coming?" she asked, gesturing at him to follow her.

William could feel his muscles pop as he stood up and began to walk out of the room.

"I don't know, Beth," William chuntered, looking down at the floor as he walked. "She looks awful. I don't remember her ever looking that bad, not even when we were kids living down South and she worked in the fields all day. I just have a bad feeling about all this." He carried on, motioning with his hands to indicate the fact that they were in a hospital to add more weight to his statement.

A teenage boy walking towards them gave William a stern look, which William barely acknowledged.

William pretended not to see the boy had gone past them.

"And this bullshit enters the fray. Mama is dying, and some lousy kid is trying to stare me down the damn hallway!"

Bethany immediately hushed him.

"Don't say things like that! Mama is not dying!" she snapped at him. "Have you talked to Dr. Boyer and Dr. Veracruz as much as I have?! You have to trust them, Will, and you've got to have faith! You're so smart, yet sometimes it's as if you know nothing." She exhaled sharply, frustrated.

"I don't know what it is that makes it so hard for you to believe they're doing the best they can, and that Mama will be fine."

They walked on until they arrived at the end of the hall, where an elevator waited. William pressed the down arrow to take them to the cafeteria that was situated on the first floor. They both waited patiently in silence until the bell dinged and the elevator door opened. Once there, they headed for the cafeteria, neither of them saying a word as they walked.

"You're a lot like Tony, you know," Bethany said with a smile as they poured hot coffee into their paper cups. "So smart, so curious," she speculated, "and sometimes, just totally unable to accept what is laid at your feet."

"Are you seriously saying I'm like your husband?" William asked, clearly surprised. "The one who splits up families for a living? Uhh, thanks, but no thanks.

I did not apply to law school to be a pawn for bitterly married assholes to use against one another," William ranted as he paid for their coffees at the cash register before heading back to their mother's room.

"Tony is a kind, courageous, loving man," Bethany retorted. "He would do anything for this family even though he only married into it. You seem to forget the times he had helped out with Mama when you were at work or studying for the LSAT," she continued, defensiveness creeping into her voice.

"He is a great father to our son and our daughter, and even with all the demands of the job he has, he still makes time for all of us. You've always liked Tony; I don't know where this sudden resentment toward him is coming from," she continued. "All he wants to do is help us: me, you, Mama, everybody. I didn't mean to hurt your feelings. I just thought it was funny that you both research something to death because you have to know it inside and out. That's all."

When they returned to the room, they ran into Dr. Boyer himself.

"Ah, Bethany! William! Coming back to see Ms. Angela? She seems to be recovering well," Dr. Boyer beamed. William bristled at the doctor's casual usage of their first names and shot an unfriendly look at him. Bethany was oblivious to the impropriety and ate it up.

"Dr. Boyer!" Bethany exclaimed, her face beaming with a wide grin. "We're so happy to hear that! I've been praying for Mama, but I knew you wouldn't let us down. After all the years she's been seeing you, I know she's been in good hands. Have you seen Dr. Veracruz?"

Before Dr. Boyer could respond, Angela stirred. William strode briskly, like a stallion, across the room to the head of her hospital bed.

"Mama?" he asked. "Mama, are you alright?"

Angela murmured again, but her words were inaudible.

"What?" Bethany said. "What is she saying, Will?"

"I don't know," William replied, then turned his gaze to Dr. Boyer.

"You know, a little privacy would be nice," he spat, narrowing his eyes at the doctor.

"William," Angela croaked. "Will—"

"Hello, Ms. Washington. How are you feeling?" Dr. Boyer boomed, ignoring William's request.

"Your levels are looking excellent. I bet you'll be running laps around the building in no time." He flashed a toothy grin at Angela, whose eyes were still not fully open. Bethany gave the doctor a polite chuckle while William scowled menacingly at him.

"Dr. Boyer?" Angela asked. "Oh. Is William here?"

"I'm right here, Mama," her son answered warmly. "How are you feeling?"

"She'll probably feel better in a few weeks," Dr. Boyer interrupted. William shot him another look.

"It would help if you gave *her* a chance to answer the question," William muttered.

"I'm so tired," Angela whispered. Despite Dr. Boyer's assurances, she still looked weary to him. William picked up her left hand, which was resting on the bed, and gently squeezed, trying not to hurt her.

"I know, Mama, but you made it through, and that's something," he replied quietly. "We're all glad for that, at least." He felt a weak smile betray his otherwise stoic expression.

"Dr. Boyer?" called Bethany. "Sorry to interrupt, but I don't remember whether or not you said you had seen Dr. Veracruz. Have you seen him?"

"Ah!" Dr. Boyer turned away from Angela and clapped his hands together. "He is with other patients today, but of course, we will be discussing your mother's case. I'm sure he'll be happy to hear that she is doing so well," he affirmed. "Now then, we will be keeping your mother here in intensive care overnight, if not for another day afterward. Then, we'll move her down to transplant care where she'll stay for a few weeks, just like we discussed before the procedure. Do you have any questions for me?" Dr. Boyer paused to be polite. When Bethany opened her mouth to speak, the doctor did not notice. "Perfect! Feel free to call my office with any questions." With a turn on his heel and a swish of his white coat, he left, closing the door behind him. Bethany sank into one of the two visitors' chairs in the room.

"He didn't give me a chance to say anything," Bethany said with a pout.

"I cannot stand that man," William grumbled, still holding Angela's hand. "He is such a phony. You see him waltzing in here like everything is just great even though Mama is not well. He couldn't even be bothered to let her say anything." He turned and looked at his mother. Her eyes had closed again.

"Mama, you still awake?" All he received were the buzzing, beeps, and whirs of the machines as a retort.

"Asleep," Bethany noted. "She's been through a lot. It's no small thing to get a new kidney, and her health was already delicate before that." She paused to take a sip of her coffee. "I know you don't like him, but Dr. Boyer is a good man. Mama loves him, and she's been seeing him for years. I mean, would you have been able to saw her open, put in a kidney, and close her back up as he did? Maybe you have to accept that there are some things that other people know better than you do." Bethany chose to let her words hang in the air as she opened her purse. She pulled out a pocket-sized volume of Scripture, opened it, and read the book silently, implying that her conversation with William was over.

William placed his mother's hand back down on the bed and crossed the room. He picked up his cup of coffee, as well as a newspaper he had purchased at the gift shop that morning and began to read.

"OVER 30 FOUND DEAD IN CALIFORNIA IN APPARENT MASS SUICIDE," the headline on the front page screamed. "INVESTIGATORS SEEKING CAUSE AND MOTIVE." Given the grim circumstances already seemingly governing his life, William opted to skip over the top news story of the day in search of lighter news. He flipped over to the sports section to read the highlights and pass the time.

About an hour passed in this manner; Angela's machines beeped while William and Bethany continued to read. The same mild-mannered nurse from before arrived again to check on Angela. This time, the vitals check woke her up.

"William? Beth?" Angela choked out. Her voice was still weak.

"We're here, Mama," William said. He folded up the paper as he rose, placing the article on the newly vacant chair. He crossed the room to be at his mother's side and noticed she was squinting.

"Beth, did you bring her glasses?"

Bethany didn't have to tell William the answer; the widening of her eyes gave her away. "Oh, God, I completely forgot. Mama, I left your glasses at my house," she said, putting her book into her bag and standing up. "I'll come up close, so you can see the both of us!" She joined William at their mother's bedside and touched her hand. "We love you, Mama!"

"My babies," Angela said, clearing her throat so that her voice would be more audible. "Goodness, how long have I been in here?"

"It's been several hours," William answered. "Doc says you're doing great."

"Which one?" Angela asked. "Dr. Boyer or Dr. Veracruz? Has Dr. Veracruz been here to see me yet?"

"Boyer. No sign of Veracruz," William said abruptly.

"But you'll be here for a few weeks," Bethany mentioned. "I'm sure he'll be able to make it by during that time. I mean, I know he is a busy man with all of his heart patients, but he has to make time for you, right, Mama?"

The word "time" spurred William to check the watch on his left wrist. The time was quarter to four. The operation itself had taken a couple of hours, and neither William nor Bethany had wanted to leave the hospital throughout the ordeal in case something happened. Remembering that he had been awake since roughly five that morning, William felt a yawn escape his mouth.

"Well, I sure don't want to be here for several weeks," Angela said, trying to sit up taller and failing to do so. "I've been sick long enough. This transplant is supposed to help!"

"Careful, Mama," William intoned softly. "You need to rest. I know that's not your nature, but you have to give yourself time." He brushed her shoulder lightly, and she sat back with a huff.

"Well, what do I do now? Sit here and wait? Where's the fun in that?" Angela grumbled.

"I brought you some puzzle books!" Bethany cried, racing back over to her pocketbook. She opened the top flap, pulling out two brightly colored paperback books and a pencil. "You know, to help the time pass! Do you want to try to do a couple?"

Angela glared at Bethany without giving her a response.

"Maybe now isn't the time, Beth," William suggested. "Maybe in a few days. We should also bring her glasses, too."

Angela muttered something barely audible, but neither of them asked her to repeat it. The tone was enough to clue them in that it was unkind.

A knock sounded from the door before it swung inward. In the doorway was Dr. Veracruz. His calm and collected demeanor was a stark contrast to Dr. Boyer's boisterous manner.

"I'm sorry to interrupt. May I come in to check on Ms. Washington?" he requested. Bethany welcomed him into the room with a nod of her head, and he closed the door behind him.

"Ms. Washington, are you awake?" he asked. In case she was asleep, he softened his voice.

"Yeah, I'm up," she replied, not as proud as she had been moments ago and still not excited. "What do you say, doc? How am I doing?"

Before giving her an answer, he reviewed the notes that he had attached to the clipboard in his hand, which annoyed William.

"Seems the transplant went well," he began.

"Glad to see you're awake. How are you feeling, Ms. Washington?"

She made a guttural sound that made him chuckle. "Well, the hard part is over. Now, we just get you back on your feet," the doctor laughed. "Not too quickly, but soon."

He moved from reviewing her paperwork to checking on her vitals on the monitors by her head. William monitored all of Dr. Veracruz's movements, similar to the way the monitor followed Angela's, and barely blinked. Bethany was less concerned and was packing the puzzle books back into her bag. Angela had her lips pursed but did not attempt to convey her thoughts to those around her.

After he was done checking the monitors and seemed satisfied with what he found, Dr. Veracruz proceeded to record something on the chart with a pen from his breast pocket.

"From what I've heard today and what I see, you look like you're on the right path, Ms. Washington," he stated, clicking the pen before placing it back into his pocket.

"I will be by again tomorrow to see you. Thank you and have a good evening," he said curtly before heading to the door.

William excused himself from the women and followed behind.

"Excuse me, doctor," he said in the hallway, chasing

behind him after closing the door. Dr. Veracruz had already begun walking away to continue his rounds.

"Dr. Veracruz!" William called. He beckoned to the doctor with his hands, interrupting the man's routine. Dr. Veracruz stopped in place and turned around.

"Yes, Mr. Washington?"

"My mom…" he began, not sure how to word the question. "Is…is she gonna be alright? It's just been tough to see her in there, and with everything that's happened, you know…" William took a breath then swallowed, finally able to gather his thoughts. "I just need to know what you think."

Forming his lips into a polite smile, Dr. Veracruz took a moment before giving his response. "Your mother is in capable hands," he finally said. "I have trusted many patients into the hands of the team here at North Suburban. We do what we can to help anyone who comes into our care," he explained in a sedate manner. "Now, please excuse me as I have to see others today. Thank you." He turned again and continued on his prior route, leaving William standing alone in the hallway.

William felt the hairs at the back of his neck prickle and instantly recognized the feeling. He remained numb for a couple of seconds as if he would be harmed if he moved even an inch. The sensation passed soon after that, and William began walking back to his mother's room. Upon entering the room, William saw that Bethany was still in the process of gathering her things.

"Mama's asleep again," Bethany said. "It's getting late, and they're going to kick us out soon anyway. Visiting hours, yadda yadda," she explained, while handing William the paper he had been reading.

"Did you want to come over for dinner tonight? Tony will be home and so will the kids. Might be nice to get your mind off of today a little bit."

"Thanks, but I think I'm gonna head home," William replied. He walked over to his sleeping mother to wish her goodbye. Leaning over, he planted a light kiss on her forehead.

"Bye, Mama," he whispered, before angling back so he was standing again. "I guess we'll be back tomorrow, right?" he asked Bethany.

"Of course," she replied, now standing still and looking at her mother. "I'll pray to God to keep her safe until we can be back tomorrow. He watched over us when we moved here so many years ago, and He got her through her surgery. I have faith that He will continue working on our behalf through the night." Her finger lingered on and fidgeted with the gold cross she wore around her neck. "G'night, Mama." Bethany opened the door and waited for her brother to follow.

"Well, I'm sorry you won't be at our house tonight, but I understand if you need some time alone," Bethany said as they walked toward the elevator.

"Thanks, Sis." They reached the elevator and William pushed the button for the ground floor. They rode the elevator with a plethora of others: scrub-clad hospital workers, visitors of varying ages and races, and a doctor who was unmistakable in her white lab coat. The majority of the group exited the elevator together on the first level and headed toward the main entrance. William and Bethany had parked beside each other, so they hugged goodbye in the lot.

"I love you," Bethany said to William, a sentiment which he returned.

"Be safe heading home. I'll see you tomorrow."

As he slid into the driver's seat of his car, William felt the twinge on his neck again. Something was coming, but he dismissed the feeling and closed his eyes before turning the key in the ignition and heading home.

CHAPTER THREE

Chicago, Illinois
March 25, 1997

His phone buzzed incessantly, tugging him back to earth. After successfully engaging in his morning prayers, ruminating on his mother's condition occupied the next hour. Something just wasn't right, and the unsettled feeling he awoke with accompanied him throughout that morning. He checked the caller ID and saw it was Bethany.

"Bethany," he said, after answering the call.

"Will! Will, the hospital just called! They said Mom isn't doing too well! Her situation suddenly worsened," she rambled woozily, taking a moment to catch her breath.

"I'm on my way to the hospital now." Will immediately cut the phone and sprang from his chair. He rushed to the door, grabbing his keys on the way. As he turned on the engine and reversed his car, he could feel the dark sensation he had been feeling all morning grow.

She's gonna be okay, he thought in an attempt to toss the feeling to the side and stay positive.

She's gonna be okay, she's gonna be okay, he kept reciting, but his chest kept getting heavier the closer he drove toward the hospital. He drove faster than he should, without caring to note how many near-red-lights he accelerated through. William arrived at North Shore Hospital in record time. He sprinted through the traffic at the entrance, ghosting past the receptionist who barked at him to slow down. He boarded the elevator with a bunch of other people who kept looking at him as though he were a madman.

"She's okay...she's okay," he kept mumbling to himself, as if those words were an anchor, stabilizing the sinking ship that was his life. The elevator finally opened, but now he walked as slowly as possible toward his mother's hospital room. As he finally reached her open door, he turned and saw Angela's lifeless body resting on the bed. He could see Bethany weeping profusely on her husband's chest while he consoled her. Tony jostled her when he saw William standing at the door as if afraid to enter. She looked at Tony, and then followed his gaze to her brother, who barely blinked. He just kept looking at his mother's face, her hair, her arms, her legs, her being.

"William!!" Bethany wailed as she ran over to hug him tightly. "She's gone! Mama's gone!!" A single tear escaped William's deadpan eyes and rolled down his cheek.

"She's...gone?" was all that escaped his lips, as if he

couldn't believe his mom was really dead. Bethany let go of her kid brother, taking one more look at her mother's corpse before falling back into her husband's arms as the sobs began anew.

He inched towards his mother's side, more tears streaming with each step. By the time he knelt by his mother's side, her dead hand on his living one, the tears flowed uncontrollably.

"Maaammaaa!!" he screamed right at his mother's face. At that moment, he never felt more unlike her. Her closed eyes and peaceful look were a sharp contrast to his reddened eyes and snotty appearance. Her hand was so cold. Why was her hand so cold? He rested his forehead on her left arm, still holding her hand.

"I…I d-don't understand how th-this happened?" he managed to say amidst the sniffs and cries. He turned to Bethany. "She was fine yesterday."

"They only said her condition got worse." It was the only reply she could muster. He could see she was barely keeping it together. She was most likely doing it because she knew he wouldn't be able to.

"Where are doctors Boyer and Veracruz?" William inquired, the calm yet ominous tone of the request making Bethany uneasy.

"William," Tony said calmly while still consoling his wife. "I don't think now's the time for—"

"Oh, now's not the time?" William snipped back, cutting Tony off before he even had a chance to finish.

"Then when is the time?! My mother just went from healthy to dead, in a day!" he shouted.

Bethany knew him all too well. Clinging to anger as a form of deflection and lashing out at anyone who would listen was something she had seen him do many times before. From the time they were kids playing outside while Mama made supper, this was William's default.

William let go of his mother's arm, clenched his fists, and was about to head outside to confront Boyer and Veracruz when a hand held him back. He knew that arm, that feeling, that love, anywhere. He felt his mother's presence and promptly turned around, a broad smile spread across his face.

"Mama?" All he saw was the same cold body he had seen all along.

"What?" Bethany asked, clearly perplexed.

"You alright there, William?" Tony asked cautiously.

"No," William replied, the smile creeping out as quickly as it had crept in. "No, I'm not."

Silence enveloped the room for the ensuing minutes.

"In all situations, we should give thanks," Bethany broke the ice. She had regained some composure by now but could see Will was still a mess. "Even though Mama is gone, we all knew the suffering she had to go through during the treatments," she continued, hoping to instill some sense of happiness into her brother. "At least now, Mama has finally found peace."

Flashes of lightning filled the sky as the rain poured heavily. The funeral church service for their mother had just concluded and everyone was headed to the internment. With their mother safely in the hearse and being transported to the graveyard, William and Bethany stood by the roadside, umbrellas in hand. Tony turned the car around and William kept Bethany company until her husband arrived. The funeral home had offered them a car, but they both refused. During that time, hordes and droves of people met with them to offer their condolences before moving on to the cemetery. Family members, friends, and acquaintances offered comforting messages and praise for Angela. William and his sister thanked them all for taking their time to come for the funeral service.

"How are you?" Bethany asked, after thanking another well-wisher.

"How do you think?" Will replied with a strained smile.

"I hate funerals," Bethany offered, taking a glance at the church with a look of dismay.

"I don't think anyone likes them." William's chest felt stiff whenever he focused on his mother's casket and he had to quickly look away. "Funerals aren't for the dead," he mused. "They're for the living. You gave a great speech, though." Her eyes were puffy, he noticed, probably due to her crying all day.

"Thanks," she replied, pausing for a while and

looking into the distance. "I hope she would have liked it."

"She sure did, watching from Heaven," Will assured. Silence surrounded them for a few minutes. William had been contemplating how to put this for a while and finally decided to blurt it out.

"Don't you think," he began cautiously, as if treading on thin ice, "that she died a bit too suddenly?" Bethany shot him a stern look. "What do you mean?" she asked menacingly, and he knew he had to phrase the next part just the right way.

"I mean, how the doctors said she was okay one minute, and she wasn't the next."

"Seriously? Right now?" Bethany glared at him, her reddish eyes making her look even scarier. "Mom is gone. If it was her time to go, then so be it. She lived a wonderful life and had two great kids. You stewing over this won't bring her back," she shot back, before facing forward with a pout, signalling the end of the conversation.

William wanted to reply but realized this wasn't the place or time when he saw another couple approaching to shake his hand and pay their respects. They waited for some minutes in silence, which was broken every now and then by an individual or group who would come to them.

"How are the kids?" she asked as Tony stood in front of them. Tony had offered to drive William's girls to the internment, a gesture he accepted and appreciated since he needed to be alone.

"They're alright. My older one keeps complaining about her back, though. We're going to check it out later this week."

"I'm sure it's nothing to worry about."

"Yeah."

He hugged his sister affectionately before she entered the car and drove off. William turned one more time, taking a long hard look through the door at the picture of his dear mother. He felt his eyes go heavy. A gush of wind ruffled his coat.

"She was a great woman," he heard someone say, and he nodded.

"Yes, she was," he replied.

"Then you should be ready to do what needs to be done," the bold voice added. Squinting his eyes and furrowing his brows, William swiftly whipped his head around to see who would say such a thing.

He realized he was the last and only person left at the church. Thinking he was going crazy, William briskly walked to his car before commencing to the internment.

The interment service was short and straight to the point. William was sure to make that clear to Pastor Reuben beforehand. His two daughters stood by his side, huddling closer to him to ward off the chill from the persistent drizzle. He looked around and saw the huge turnout, people he barely recognized, looking sad or weeping. Mama truly had touched a lot of lives. William couldn't help but smile while thinking of all the good Mama had probably done in these people's lives. He felt a slight nudge and looked to his right; his eyes met with a concerned look from Bethany. She could tell he wasn't paying attention to Pastor Reuben's speech, which annoyed her.

"What're you smiling for?" she whispered.

"It was a good idea making this service accessible to everyone," he whispered back, gesticulating at the crowd of Angela-admirers. Bethany looked around and was shocked at the number of people Mama knew. She also smiled.

"As we say our final goodbyes to our sister, Angela," Pastor Reuben said as he approached the end of his brief sermon, "Bethany and William would like to thank all of you again for taking the time to be here today. We will conclude our memorial service with a prayer." The attendees bowed their heads in respect as the pastor led them in worship. As William looked at his folded hands, he felt the familiar prickle at the back of his neck that had bothered him off and on since his childhood in Mississippi.

"Amen," they all said in unison at the end of the prayer.

"There will be a reception for family members of Angela at the home of her daughter, Bethany," Pastor Reuben concluded. "May God be with all of you today."

With the dissolution of the formalities, the

funeral-goers gave generous hugs to one another. Now that the general public had access, even more people came to meet Angela's two kids.

"She loved you so much."

"We talked about you often."

"I'm sure you will miss her."

Everyone had something good to say about Angela. The number of people that rushed them at the cemetery made the numbers at the church pale in comparison. William, however, never minded, as long as they were praising his beloved mother. When leaving the graveyard, he turned and looked one more time at his mother's tombstone. On it was inscribed, "*HERE LIES ANGELA WASHINGTON. LOVING MOTHER, SISTER, GRANDMOTHER, AND FRIEND.*" He felt the back of his head prickle yet again, putting him on guard.

"You need to be ready for what's to come," the same voice bellowed into his ear, making him react animatedly. People stared at him with scowls, unsure what to make of his antics.

At his sister's place, William secluded himself in the backyard after securing some culinary chops on a plate for himself, but not before checking in on his girls. He saw they were playing with their cousins, already forgetting the somber occasion. In the backyard, two men stood smoking at the corner. William decided to sit as far away from them as possible in an attempt to avoid the nauseating smell. He took a moment to reminisce about all the things he loved about his Mama: her cooking, her lessons, and her smile. He closed his eyes, privately reminiscing about all their good times together. When he got into and graduated from both high school and college, she had been by his side; her infectious smile was always with him. He had applied to Harden Law School, but a part of him didn't care if he got in because he knew Mama could not follow him there.

"She was a good woman who really loved you," the voice said softly.

William felt uneasy but replied nonetheless, "Yes. Yes, she was." His eyes remained closed.

"Which is why you need to fight for her."

William's eyes shot wide open and looked around but could see no one. "Sp... Spector?"

"It has been a while, William," the ominous, powerful voice chimed.

"What do you mean by I need to fight for her? My mother is dead!"

"Do you think she died of natural causes?" Spector asked. William pondered this for a couple of seconds. "Or do you think there is more to it?" Spector finalized. William's eyes widened, and he realized his gut feeling hadn't been for nothing.

"Do you know something I don't?" William asked hastily. Silence.

"Spector?" Silence, yet again, retorted.

William had not forgotten Spector since his early encounter with him thirty-seven years ago. A part of him had chalked it up to his imagination, but he also felt it was more than that. Although Will had neither seen nor spoken to the ghoulish entity since that day, the timing was impeccable. He remembered the day after the incident: his mother packing him and Bethany into their car, driving them for hours northward to Illinois. He recalled how his father had awakened moments before they left, begging his mother not to go and insisting he would make changes. He recalled the way his father's hands shook as Angela stayed firm and refused to change her mind. The move had a significant impact on altering their family and greatly influenced their destiny.

"Good to see you, Will," muttered Uncle Earl, one of the smokers and the elder brother of William's late mother. "Wish it was for a different reason." William nodded at him as he went back into the house, leaving William alone outside.

"WHAT'RE YOU THINKING about, silly?" William forgot he had zoned out again. He had been thinking about what Spector told him. Months had passed, but he had not made any significant progress on the matter. It would help if Spector had come to fully explain what he meant and lead him to who might have been responsible for his mother's demise. He had no leads, nothing to go on, and no concrete evidence of foul play leading to her kicking the bucket.

"Hello-o-o!" Bethany called to her brother again, waving in his face. "Anybody home?" she asked jokingly.

"Ha-ha, funny," William replied bluntly, and Bethany giggled.

"You know you should really have some fun," Bethany enounced. "It's the last day of the year. A new year is on the horizon!"

"And what's so great about this year to be thankful for?" William shot back, and Bethany sighed.

"I know it's been a hard year for all of us, you especially," she started, placing a hand on her brother's arm. "Esther's surgery must have been hard. You chose not to go to Harden for your children, and Mom died," she explained. "But in all situations, we should give thanks," she noted. "You got a promotion, I'm about to start my real estate project, and even though you didn't choose to go, you were accepted into Harden Law School. But most importantly..." Bethany held her brother's hand with both of hers. "...We are all alive. Esther, Kayla, Jacob, Lindsey, Tony, you, and I are all alive." She said each name with an added weight to make him truly appreciate that they weren't just names, but family. A loud roar filled the living room, and they simultaneously looked over to see what was up. It was 12:00 (midnight) and the beginning of 1998.

"Happy New Year, Sis."

"Happy New Year, Will."

CHAPTER FOUR

Chicago, Illinois
December 2, 1998

WILLIAM OPENED HIS eyes and sat up abruptly, waking up from his dream. He clicked the clock on his bedside table and saw the time was 1 am. Standing, he stretched his legs and went to check on his girls. After seeing that they were alright, he strolled down to the kitchen, pouring himself a glass of water to help clear his head. He got back to his room and noticed the light entering through the window. Moving closer to his window, he gazed at the moon, enamored by its light. Such a view affected him in a surreal way, and in a flash, all his memories of the dream that caused him to wake up began flooding his mind.

He remembered being surrounded by blood, seemingly endless in supply. He wasn't personally covered or tainted by any of the blood, but from where he stood, he could see a good number of people sinking through the blood into the depths below. They kept crying and screaming for help, but no one came to their aid. As he looked further, he could see a cloaked figure floating above the water. Sinking beside the ghost-like creature was his mother, Angela.

"Mama!" he screamed, trying to run to her but unable to move.

"You'll drown too, if you come any closer," the cloaked creature pointed out, his thunderous voice bellowing and leaving echoes.

"Then do something!" William retorted in anger, trying to plead with the ghoul to no avail. Slowly but surely, Angela was engulfed by the blood, and the only thing William could do was watch in agony.

"Jesus Christ," he said to himself after remembering his dream, making the sign of the cross. William went back to bed but couldn't shake off a mysterious feeling that he was in store for something later that morning, even though he could not quite figure out what. Could it be from his neighbors? Unlikely. The newspaper? That seemed the most plausible. He pondered on it for a few minutes before ultimately deciding he needed sleep now, so he could be awake then if anything happened.

William got up at precisely 7:33 am and cursorily went about his morning routine. He then woke his daughters up so they could prepare for school. From his room, he could see the young kid who delivered newspapers riding through the neighborhood. He flung a copy of the morning paper at William's front porch. He sped downstairs, swiftly opening the door and taking his paper, then closing the door behind him. William decided to first check the main topics before reading the rest. He scanned through them while going to the kitchen to get his coffee. The main headline almost made him choke on his coffee and drop the mug. It read: '*Years Later, 40,000 Warned of Possible Transfusion Risk.*'

He carefully walked to and took a seat on a cushioned chair in the living room, resting his coffee mug on the saucer sitting on the stool beside him. He still couldn't believe it.

"*An estimated thirty-five to forty thousand people may have received tainted blood transfusions or supplies at 28 Chicago-area hospitals between June 1994 and December 1996. The blood may not have been properly tested for HIV or hepatitis viruses…*" he read, still shocked at what stared him in the face. He heard a loud thump upstairs, which made him remember he still had to drive his kids to school.

"Girls!! Time for school!" he called to his daughters.

On the way to school, William could not get his mind off the newspaper article. He hadn't found ample time, or any time for that matter, to dig into it. His eyes kept alternating between the road and the newspaper by his side while his daughters rambled on about school. He promptly dropped them off and sped away before they could get a word in. His mind was on other things at the moment. A lot of things.

He arrived back home, took a seat, and finally read

up on the article. As he went through the immensely detailed anecdote, he realized some things were not right and came to understand what had caused his mother's death. The article posited many people had been infected at hospitals and listed all the years such people were infected. Succeeding their names and years were the consequential hospitals in which they received treatment and care. Will's mouth gaped open, and his eyes widened in a mix of horror and anger as he noted Christopher and North Shore hospitals as two of the hospitals giving tainted blood to people. Both hospitals had overseen the blood transfusion process his deceased mother received. He remembered Mama had gotten her blood transfusions on the 6th, 9th, 10th, 13th, and 15th of November, 1996.

"If they were contaminated…" he whispered to himself, his eyes growing even bigger. He was finally connecting the dots; his dream this morning, what Spector had told him, his suspicions—they were all pointing to this. He turned his gaze and full attention back to the newspaper he had in his hand and kept reading, his eyes fixated like they were going to bore a hole through the paper. The paper stated the blood products necessary for the transfusions in question were administered between 1994 and 1996. He knew for a fact they were wrong on this number.

"This is ridiculous!" he screamed. "Any of these calculations could be off by a margin. Over one hundred thousand people could have been affected by this," William continued to himself. He surmised, from all he had read, that his mother had most likely been contaminated during one of the five blood transfusions she received at the hospitals. This could explain her several relapses. He knew exactly who to blame next.

"That damn Boyer!" he groaned out in frustration, squeezing the sides of the newspaper he held. He wasn't sure if both Boyer and Veracruz knew about this, but he was willing to bet they did. William knew he didn't have the full story. For all he knew, they could have found out the blood was contaminated and provided several more transfusions to try rectifying the problem without telling the patient or her loved ones.

"*Because of the serious nature of improper testing, the FDA has no assurance that blood samples from September 1, 1991, through November 20, 1996, were properly tested,*" he read straight from the article audibly, as if trying to make sense of it all despite already having made sense of it. He kept reading the piece over and over again until his kids had returned from school. He barely acknowledged them. There was food in the fridge, so he was sure they wouldn't need him anytime soon. He continued re-reading every sentence until it was 7 pm. After countless hours, the truth eventually became evident and clear to William. He was still not sure of anything and thought this could all just be in his head. All he had were suspicions and dreams; he had no actual reason to feel the doctors mistreated Mama besides his gut feeling.

He needed to go to North Shore Hospital to see his mother's medical records. He wanted to call Bethany, but he couldn't do that without proof. It would be unfair to her for him to bring out old wounds about Mama's death with no concrete evidence. He got in his car and drove to the hospital. When he got there, the medical records clerk immediately recognized him because of his frequent visits to the hospital.

"Welcome, Mr. Washington," she said cautiously, with a weak smile. "I'm sorry about your mother."

"Thank you. I would like to request my mother's medical records of her time here," he said, which startled the clerk. "I would also appreciate it if you would bring the records this hospital acquired from Christopher Hospital about my mother," he explained calmly.

"All right, please wait over there," the clerk instructed, pointing at the waiting area.

William sat, waiting impatiently. Sitting in the two seats beside him, a mother and daughter noticed the ferocity with which he vibrated his leg. When the documents finally arrived, he grabbed them in his hands quickly, startling the clerk. He scoured through them with a ferocious appetite. After reading to his satisfaction, he returned the files to her. William walked out of the hospital coolly and headed straight for his sister's house.

"Knock! Knock!"

"Who is it?!" Bethany asked in an overly cautious manner.

"It's Will."

The door was promptly unlocked. Will counted the unlocking of three distinct locks before the door opened.

"Will, hi!" Bethany beamed at him. "You never just come unannounced."

That was true; he never did. She gestured him to come in before closing the door behind her. Bethany looked at him carefully after getting a glass of water for him at his request. He looked unhinged and somewhat agitated. His fists were clenched and he kept panting like he had run a marathon.

"What's wrong, Will?" she asked, clearly serious now from her tone. She took a seat while he gathered his thoughts.

"I know you're not going to want to hear this," he began with a cautious approach, trying to let her know she needed to be prepared before hearing him. "I think the hospitals caused Mama's death. I know what you are going to say, but read this article."

He shoved the newspaper he had been holding on to throughout the day towards her. She was stunned but decided to give him the benefit of the doubt and viewed it.

"This is awful," she said while reading it.

"Exactly!" William concurred. She kept reading until she was done.

"You do know this doesn't prove anything, right?" she put it bluntly to him.

He knew that too, which was why he had gone to

the hospital to find proof. Even though he found some things that were very useful, they were all circumstantial. He still needed to tell someone, and she was the best person he could tell.

"I know, which was why I went to the hospital to request Mama's records. I—"

"You what?!"

"Yes! I read her records from both Christopher and North Shore. I—"

"Have you gone senile?!"

"Will you just let me finish, Beth?"

Bethany went silent, waiting for him to make his case.

"I found out from the records that Mama had only become sick after her blood transfusions began," he explained while Bethany folded her arms. "The transfusions affected her worse at Christopher than they did at North Shore."

Bethany just glared at him, hands still crossed.

"So?" she asked bluntly.

"I know it's not much, and I don't even know what to think myself, but Mama's death could have been caused by the hospitals."

"Will, what do you hope to gain by doing this?" she inquired, walking closer to him. "You need to let this go."

He buried himself on the cushion chair nearby. He noticed a creak on the floor from the hallway.

"Is someone else here?" he asked cautiously.

"No, the kids are with Tony. He took them to buy some ice cream not long ago. He'll be back soon," she explained.

This worried Will because he heard another creak of the timber floor.

"Do you hear that?" William whispered to Bethany, and she nodded. The fear was apparent in her eyes and face.

"I didn't lock the door."

"What?"

"I didn't lock the door," she repeated herself. "Our neighborhood isn't as safe as it once was. So, Tony got more locks."

She had been too preoccupied with Will's somber mood to bother locking the door.

"Stay behind me," Will said to Bethany, and she obeyed.

A burly man walked out of the shadows of the hallway, a black hood covering his worn face. He held a gun in his hand, which made Bethany even more scared. She wanted to scream but quickly covered her mouth with her hands.

"Smart girl," the hooded man commended, pointing the gun at them both.

"Look, if it's money you want, I have some," William tried to negotiate. "Take my wallet. Take everything in it." He slowly used his hands to get his wallet out of his back pocket and showed the robber.

"Bring it over here," the robber commanded in his husky voice. "And leave the lady over there." William did as he asked. The robber slowly picked it up and confirmed there was indeed money in there, making him smirk.

"Thanks for the donation, but I didn't come here to rob," he explained. Both siblings exchanged perplexed glances before returning their gaze to the hooded man. "I came here to kill."

"What?!" Will shouted. By now Bethany was shedding tears.

"Your husband put the wrong guy in jail," said the man in a lofty tone, pointing the gun at Bethany. William could hear sirens outside, but he really couldn't think about that right now. "His brother has sent me to repay the favor tenfold." He pulled the trigger.

All William could remember was falling hard, as if the whole world fell with him...on him. He could hear Bethany crying and moving her lips but couldn't make out what she was saying. The last thing he saw was the hooded man running from the police and Tony rushing to Bethany's side. William slowly closed his eyes. He could feel the pain in his stomach, which was wet, along with his hand. As William Washington closed his eyes completely and gave in to the dark abyss, he finally remembered: he had jumped in the way.

CHAPTER FIVE

North Suburban Hospital
Chicago, Illinois
December 12, 1998

"SOMEBODY, PLEASE HELP!!!" William could hear faintly to his left. He had been in and out of consciousness since he'd been shot. He recognized that voice.; it was his sister's. He could still feel wet, but a hand was placed on his side, most likely to reduce the bleeding by applying pressure on the wound. He grimaced when he felt a thump at the back of his head. He was on a rolling bed. He managed to pry his eyes open and immediately squinted them due to the bright bulbs emitting light in the hospital. After taking a moment to readjust his vision, he saw a nurse talking with a frantic Bethany. Tony was also there, covered in blood. His blood.

"What happened?!" he could hear the nurse ask as he began to lose consciousness again. His eyelids wavered up and down as he tried to fight the sensation. "And where is Dr. Henry?!"

"He was shot!" Beth replied, in tears. "He was protecting me!"

"B-Beth?" William barely said. Bethany quickly shot her eyes down and noticed he was partially awake.

"Will! Will!!" she shouted as two nurses rolled him through the hallway and into the ER.

"You're gonna have to wait here, ma'am," the nurse explained calmly.

"He's gonna be okay, right?!" she asked, sweating profusely. Tony stood by her side to comfort her.

"I can't promise that, ma'am, but I can tell you we will do everything in our power to keep him alive," the nurse replied warmly before walking briskly into the room.

"He's gonna be okay, right, Tony?" Beth turned to ask her husband. Tony looked into her eyes. He wanted to give her a realistic answer due to habit from being a lawyer, but when he saw her eyes, eyes begging for a yes, he merely nodded and hugged her tight.

"He's going to be okay, dear," he encouraged, rubbing her back with his palm while she sobbed. "It's all going to be all right."

Will opened his eyes again. He squinted them as a reflex to the bright bulb directly facing him from above. Pushing it to the side, Will looked around and realized he was in the hospital, lying in the Emergency Room.

He sat up quickly, whipping his head left and right like a guard dog. William looked down to check his gunshot wound but could only see skin, which shocked and confused him. He could hear a steady beep in his head but couldn't tell where it was coming from. Feeling the place where his injury once was, he came down from the operation bed; his shirt was still stained with blood in numerous places. He walked out of the Emergency Room but couldn't see anyone.

"Hello?!" he called. "Is anybody here?!" Silence responded to his calls, which only served to leave him more confused.

"What the heck is going on?" William muttered to himself, his eyebrows angled in a mixture of annoyance and confusion. The hairs on the back of his neck began tingling, giving him an all-too-familiar sensation. He turned around but saw no one. Reaching his hand up to feel his neck, Will felt the urge to go up the elevator, as if some nebulous force was calling out to him. He walked slowly to the elevator, boarded it, and set it for the second floor.

His back remained stuck to the wall at all times during the seemingly endless ride. He could still hear the beeping, but it was somewhat slower than before, or was it? He didn't have time to think about it. William quickly got off the elevator, and for the first time, noticed he was on the floor where his mother's hospital ward was. A feeling lured him to her ward. He walked as slowly and cautiously as possible. Until he understood exactly what this was, he would not let his guard down.

As he got closer to Angela's ward, he could feel the force become stronger and stronger. When he had reached her room, William could see a lurid light emanating from it. He proceeded to enter and saw his dear mother sitting on her bed, similar to the last time he had seen her.

"Took you long enough to find us, boy," she remarked with a smirk. He sprinted like he was in a hundred-meter race, landing on his mother with a grand hug. She laughed and returned the gesture.

"M-Mama? How…"

"Let's not worry about that right now," Angela replied, nodding her head in a direction behind him. He promptly turned and saw Spector standing at the edge of the room. He could barely see any discerning features of the ghost. Only a cloak, of which darkness utterly filled where his head should have been visible, was discernable. William assumed there was a body hidden in that long dark cloak; there had to be.

"Now you show up," Will noted, rolling his eyes in annoyance.

"Now, don't be upset, Will," his mother chided. "Mr. Spector over here is the reason we can speak now."

"Huh, is that so?"

"Yes, it is, William." Spector's huge voice filled the air, echoing not only through the walls, but vibrating through William's being. It was as if the ghost's power was stronger here.

"Where am I?" William inquired. "Am I dead?"

"You are at the point between life and death," Spector explained. "The tipping point. You have not yet fully crossed over but slowly, you are."

William could still hear the beeping. He was sure it was slower now.

"Your friend was able to bring me from the dead to this place so that we could talk for a little while," Angela elaborated further, her son listening attentively. "And I think you know what this is about, or at least suspect it," she added. William's face became serious. He turned his gaze momentarily to Spector, then back to his mother.

"Mama—" He paused to let out a cough. "Did those doctors, Boyer and Veracruz, cause your death?" He went straight to it, airing out his suspicions.

"You're asking the wrong question," Spector noted. Angela smiled as Will looked at them both in a confused fashion.

"What do you mean?"

"It's not just about me, dear," Angela mused, holding her boy's hand tightly. "It's about a whole lot of people." The boldness and seriousness laced in her tone told him this was a grievous matter.

"You're talking about the tainted blood, aren't you?"

"You've finally caught on," Spector commended. "You need to uncover the truth about the thousands of innocent people that have been, and are being, infected by a tainted blood supply from these hospitals."

"So, it is true," William pondered, whispering to

himself. His eyes immediately lit up and he swiftly turned to his mother.

"Were you one of them, Mama?"

"Who knows?" she replied, which did not satisfy William. "I could have been. I might not have been. I don't know for sure."

William furrowed his brows, slightly perplexed by the whole scenario.

"Being dead doesn't make me know everything, you know," she added. "But that's why I have you," Angela said softly, placing her hand on his cheek. "I can rest easy knowing you will not do the same until the cause of my death is revealed."

William smiled. He was so glad that his mother wanted him to do this. Part of the reason he had not followed up on his suspicions was that he didn't think his mother would want him going after people who he wasn't sure were responsible. He held her hand again; how he wished Bethany was here for this moment.

"Tell my daughter I love her," Angela chimed. "It's her job now to keep you out of trouble."

"I will, Mama," assured Will.

"Your mission isn't only for your mother," Spector interjected with his brazen voice. "It is also for the others, living and dead, who need you to bring justice and prevent others from being infected."

"The issue of tainted blood began earlier than 1994," Spector began his soliloquy, explaining the full details of the case to William, who was not surprised by this statement. William had suspected this but was glad to have confirmation.

"It was understandable that they would rather not inform the public to prevent panic or an outcry, but it was necessary for them to have told those who were infected and had received sullied transfused blood. It was their duty."

William was stunned by this revelation and his mouth remained wide open. How could they have done this? Did these people not care for the patients who would bear the actual cost of their mistakes?

"The faulty testing was performed by the New Hope Blood Center, which screens blood for Chicago Blood Services, popularly known as UBS. While the Chicago Blood Services provided blood supplies to hospitals in eighteen states, only the blood sent to hospitals in Chicago, Pittsburgh, Memphis, and New York was affected," Spector went on.

"While the FDA and CDC communicated their concerns to one another, the blood supplier and the owner of the blood products sent to the hospitals did not alert the individuals or the public promptly," continued Spector. "They probably had their reasons, but none that would be a viable excuse."

William could hear the beeps in his head getting slower and fainter. He wondered what it was but decided to leave that for later. He wanted to get as much knowledge as possible now.

"In 1981, only four cases of AIDS were reported. Over twenty-thousand AIDS cases had been reported between the years 1982 and 1998. Some were related to tainted blood transfusions, and the majority came from the Chicago area. From 1990 to 1998, more than 13,000 cases of AIDS were reported in Cook County and Chicago," Spector continued, but this left William perplexed.

"Wait. What does AIDS have to do with it?" He stopped Spector's monologue to make his inquiry.

"During the tainted blood crisis between 1990 and 1996, there had been an escalation of AIDS cases. In 1990, 942 cases were reported, rising in 1994 to 2,462, and dropping to 962 in 1998," Spector answered, his echoes reverberating all over the room.

"For example, the FDA received inquiries concerning a recall of blood products by the Greater New Hope Blood Program in New York City. The blood products, which initially tested reactive for the HIV antibody, an indication of the presence of the virus that causes AIDS, were not tested in duplicate, as required by the manufacturer's testing instructions and FDA regulations. The recalled blood products were collected on March 15, 1987, and included red blood cells, platelets—a blood component used to aid clotting—and recovered plasma. The donor responded that he had tested HIV-1 positive in April 1992," Spector detailed with a suitable sobriety to better convey the situation to William.

Just then, William felt weaker. He could feel the

blood peeling from his skin as the injury began to resurface. He could hear the beeping getting fainter and fainter, the intervals between each beep becoming longer and longer.

"What is that beeping?" he asked while slumping on his mother's thighs, now physically unable to move.

"What beeping? What's happening?" Angela, clearly concerned for her child's safety, inquired to Spector.

"His body is weakening. The doctors are losing him. He has to leave now," Spector elaborated on the present situation. "Sorry, William, but you will have to make do with what you have learned up till now," Spector lamented.

Raising his hands to the sky, he began a prayer to God.

"Oh, Lord, send your beloved child back to the living to finish the work he was meant to do. Let him be a beacon of hope and save many lives in Your name and glory. Have mercy on him and hear my prayer, Lord. Let him go back and be a loving father to his children, a caring brother to his sister, and a dear friend to all his colleagues and compatriots. It is not his time, oh Lord. Lord, hear my prayer and allow him to go back to the land of the living! In Jesus' name, Amen."

For each sentence Spector said, William could hear the beep getting slightly louder, with shorter intervals between each beep. He knew he was leaving, making him hold on to his Mama's hand while she rocked his hair with her other one.

"I love you, William," she said quietly. He squeezed her hand tight as if he never wanted to be departed from her ever again.

"Tell your sister I love her, too," she added, making him grin.

"And tell Tony to take care of my baby girl better," she said, more as a warning than a request. The beeps sounded like they were getting closer, now quite audible.

"Bye, Mama."

William opened his eyes and inhaled deeply, taking in all of the air he possibly could. He squinted his eyes at the light bulb directly above him yet again before looking around and realizing he was back in the Emergency Room, surrounded by a doctor and two nurses with masks covering their noses. He could hear the beeps clearly now and turned to see that it was his heart rate.

"Vitals are stable," William could hear the doctor say calmly. As the doctor and nurses checked some of his other vitals and packed up the surgery equipment, he wondered about what he had just witnessed and experienced during the surgery. William knew it was time to take action.

CHAPTER SIX

Chicago, Illinois
1999

"**B**UT IF YOU could just…" the respondent hung up, causing William to groan and fling his phone at the couch. He fell back on his chair. That was the fourth attorney he had contacted who immediately backed down the moment he heard Will was going after the hospitals. The person he had just conversed with spoke to the complexities of the case as the reason for his refusal to work on the case, but Will knew that was nonsense. He, and all the other lawyers, seemed afraid of going against the blood bank doctors that would be on the opposing end of the argument.

To make matters worse, the statute of limitations on the case would soon be up; on the 25th of March to be exact. He had no time to wait for an attorney. If they were all afraid, he'd rather do it himself. He heard a knock on the door and stood to see who it was. William felt a slight pain in his torso as he got up, a reminder that his gunshot wound had not yet fully healed.

"Who is it?" William asked as he approached the door.

"It's Beth." He heard his sister's voice from the other side of the door, spurring him to open it and let her in.

"You look like crap," she noted with a smirk on her face, but she wasn't wrong. She could see his baggy eyes, pointing to minimal sleep.

"Why aren't you sleeping on your bed?" she asked, noting the small indents on his face and arms showing his penchant for sleeping on rough or hard surfaces.

"Most times I fall asleep while working."

Bethany shook her head in disapproval. He had just survived a gunshot wound. She had begged him to take some rest, but he didn't listen. Instead, he worked long hours researching a conspiracy that wasn't there. She had been coming to see him as regularly as possible. She knew he needed all the help he could get right about now, with his kids and his new-found obsession. Even though she didn't believe him, she felt she still had to support him and watch over him while he went on this ludicrous quest.

She walked through the hallway into the living room and was shocked to see so many books spread around to different areas of the room. She turned and scowled at him, but he just walked past her to have a seat.

"What the heck is this?" she inquired, her tone laced

with a mix of anger and confusion. "These weren't here when I came over two days ago."

"Well, I had to intensify my search since the deadline for the statute of limitations is coming up soon," Will explained, pausing to take a sip from his coffee. "Both on a lawyer and the hospitals."

"You can't keep doing this to yourself," Bethany advised, trying to arrange the mess that was his living room. "You need to rest. It's already 2pm."

"Two? Already?" he exclaimed, rising from his chair. "I've got to go to the library," he said to Bethany, waving at her and exiting his house to her utter surprise.

Roughly two months later, and two days before the statute of limitations was to expire, William Washington filed a complaint in the United States District Court Northern District of Illinois Eastern Division with case number 88 C 1777. Coming out of the building, a sense of satisfaction came over him. Even though he had still not yet found an attorney for his case, Will believed he had made one giant step towards uncovering the truth and making those who were responsible pay. His phone rang, and he saw it was Beth.

"So, everything went as planned, right?" she asked after he answered her call.

"Yes," he replied. "I feel like a new attorney filing his first case." Will mused, looking up to the sky with a broad smile.

"That's good and all, but you do know you still need to get an attorney for your case," she cautioned. "You can't go up against the hospitals all by yourself. Heck, even with an attorney your chances are still not that great."

"Yeah, thanks for ruining the mood, Beth," he said bluntly, causing her to chuckle.

After hanging up the call, William went straight to the library to do more research on similar cases and their outcomes. Throughout his research process, he always felt like there was something guiding him to the right places and the right cases. Was it Spector, perhaps? Or was he reading too much into it?

As the first court date approached, William searched tirelessly for an attorney to represent him. A small number of attorneys considered taking on the case but he could not wait for them, as the day he would appear in court was now closer than ever. William was able to send subpoenas to all of the defendants who he would need to testify in the case. After making sure he had served the defendants their summons, he knew he needed to focus all of his energy on finding an attorney. Bethany might be skeptical, but she did have a solid point; he couldn't do it alone. He needed help.

"Hello?"

William decided to contact an attorney who had been handling a real estate matter for him. He told the attorney about the specifics of the case he had filed and asked if he was interested. He needed someone who was not only right but also passionate about what he was trying to achieve with the case.

"Uhmm…okay, go on," the man at the other side of the phone urged.

William began explaining the specifics of his case to Mr. Harper. After detailing all of the facets of the case as best he could, the lawyer told him to give him a couple of days to think about it.

A few days later, Mr. Harper informed William he was interested in handling the case.

"Are you sure?" William asked the man cautiously, squinting his eyes as if not sure about Harper's motivations.

"Yes!" Harper replied briskly, which startled William. "Look, I have handled cases like this before. We just have to destroy their credibility as an upstanding hospital while keeping ours."

William could see he seemed excited about the prospect of the case. This was precisely the kind of partner he had hoped to find. Mr. Harper filed his appearance with the Federal Court so that he would be seen as the attorney of record, and they spent the next two months working on how they would go about the case in and out of court.

William opened his eyes and looked around. He had gone to sleep early that night and was lying on his bed, rubbing his eyes in an attempt to see clearer. He turned to check the time but saw it was blank, which perplexed him.

"William," a bold, powerful voice beckoned to him. It made him shake just at the sheer power the voice carried. He knew who it was. He had heard that voice all too many times, but while he could hear the voice, he could not see its owner.

"Spector?" he called. The shadowy ghoul came out of the darkness at the corner of the room, his cloak seemingly floating at the edges like embers from a fire.

"Where am I? Is this a dream?" he asked.

"Yes, William," Spector answered.

"What's going on? Do you have something to tell me?" William inquired.

"Yes," Spector retorted. "An act has been done behind your back. Something has been carried out without your knowledge or permission," he boomed.

"What do you mean? What is it?"

"The lawyer you hired has dismissed the case he was handling for you," Spector informed.

"What?! He dismissed my case against the blood bank hospitals?!"

"No," Spector corrected, moving closer to where Will was now sitting on his bed. "He dismissed your other case."

"The real estate case?"

"Yes, William. The man dismissed it without your knowledge. Do you think you can trust him?"

"Then who do I..." William woke up before he could finish his statement, whipping his head left and right in an attempt to gauge where he was. He had just woken up from his dream, lying on his bed, and he knew the purpose of Spector's visit. That message from the ghost, he believed, was a warning that his current case against the hospitals was in jeopardy as well.

"Could he have done that?" William pondered on his dream. He didn't think Spector was lying, but it just seemed so ludicrous that an attorney would dismiss a case without the knowledge or permission of his or her client. A strong wind blew from the window and his lamp flew to the other side of the room before his very eyes. He couldn't believe what he was seeing. Immediately after that, the calendar forcibly fell off the wall of its own volition.

"Okay, okay, I get it!" Will shouted into nothingness, indicating he understood Spector was dead serious about William needing to heed his warnings. He was both baffled and scared at the events that had just unfolded. However, the court date was only two days away. He still needed to verify and be sure.

Eventually, William checked with the courts to gauge the veracity of what Spector had said and indeed, he was right, as always. William found out his attorney, Mr. Harper, had dismissed the real estate case last year.

"Unbelievable," he muttered to himself. He wanted to call Mr. Harper but a force made him feel that was a bad idea. He surmised it was too soon since he was outraged now and might do or say something ill-advised. William could still not fathom that this was the same man who had called him in February of this year to tell him the real estate case would soon go to trial.

How could a lawyer so blatantly lie to his client about something so serious? Later in the day, he called his attorney.

"Hello, William."

"Mr. Harper, I just wanted to call and see if you have all you need for the big day tomorrow." William had decided not to mention to Harper his knowledge of the real estate case until tomorrow.

"Yes, of course," the attorney replied, a little louder than Will would have appreciated. "I have all my documents; all of the witnesses are ready. We're good to go," he assured, which just left a sour taste in William's mouth.

"Alright then, till tomorrow."

"Alright William; 'bye."

William Washington arrived early at the Federal Court building the next morning to ensure that everything was going according to plan. When he saw Mr. Harper, the bad taste in his mouth came again and he felt like insulting him, but instead, he remained calm. He looked at the way his attorney dressed and compared it to his own blue suit and black briefcase. He looked like the actual lawyer of the two of them, which made him even less confident in Mr. Harper's capabilities.

By 9:30 am, William and his attorney were in court and the proceedings were about to begin. Before the clerk called his case, William had turned back to get a feel of the courtroom and who was in attendance. He counted just over twenty people seated in the room; twenty-two to be exact. A few minutes later, the clerk called his case, Slaughter v. New Hope Blood Center et al. After the case was called, eighteen people stood up and approached the bench, leaving only four people sitting.

"Are they…all lawyers?" he murmured to himself in amazement. Was this what he was going up against? He couldn't believe the number of defendants' lawyers that had come to the hearing. Some defendants even had two attorneys representing their doctors and hospitals. William had always known he was going to be in for the legal battle of his life, but only then did he understand the gravity of what that meant.

For the first time in a while, real doubt crept into his mind. He was not sure if he could win against all of these lawyers. He had spent almost all of his remaining insurance money on the case. He turned to Mr. Harper and remembered he didn't even have a lawyer that he could trust. Should he quit? Could he even win if he kept on fighting?

His mind kept wandering all over the place while the judge talked, and the attorneys responded. As they spelled their names for the court reporter, a defense attorney wearing an expensive suit moved cautiously to where William stood.

"Hey, look, I am going to blow this case away," he said in a menacing voice, looking straight at William. He continued to stare him down for several long moments. William knew it was merely a tactic to intimidate and demoralize him. William felt defeated. He was on the verge of quitting and going home to his kids. William closed his eyes and took a deep breath.

"Oh, God, please help me," he whispered, and almost instantly, he felt invigorated. He started feeling powerful and his conviction was reaffirmed. He smiled, much to his attorney's surprise, and decided never to allow himself to be afraid, belittled, or intimidated by the attorneys ever again.

"I know the motions to dismiss will be many, so please don't wait until the last minute," the judge said after the attorneys had finished speaking. He set the next status hearing for June 16, 1999.

William remained seated after most people had exited the courtroom. He was wondering why he didn't fire Harper on the spot. Eventually, he got up to leave. As he was exiting the courtroom, he saw his attorney by a corner down the hall. He was colluding with a few of the defendants' lawyers. When he saw their facial expressions after they realized he had seen them, he understood they didn't want him to know about the discourse they were engaged in. It was then that everything became clear.

He was too angry to confront his attorney and didn't want to make a scene, especially in court. It was then he believed his dream entirely. Mr. Harper had informed him he didn't even have to appear in court, and that he would handle everything. Had "handling everything" included selling out? Because it sure looked like that's what his attorney was doing. Mr. Harper's motives were now clear and obvious for William to see.

CHAPTER SEVEN

June 15, 1999
Illinois

"Hello?"

"William, hi," Mr. Harper greeted before getting into what he wanted. "I wanted to inform you that I would need some money as payment for working on this case," he explained, which annoyed William.

What had he done? For all he knew, Harper was not an ally, but instead already conniving with the blood bank lawyers.

"We should meet up. There are some things about our agreement that should be changed," William replied curtly. They agreed to meet up at the attorney's office. When he arrived, William presented Mr. Harper with a contract that stated, among other things, that their agreement was on a contingency basis when Mr. Harper agreed to take the case. While the lawyer ruminated over the details of the agreement, William continued to wonder why he was requesting money all of a sudden.

Mr. Harper knew Will was aware of the contingency agreement, which was why Will felt baffled.

Harper promptly signed the agreement after digesting its contents sufficiently and handed it back over to him.

"Do you have a check for me?" he asked as William collected the contract agreement.

"I'll call you later," William replied, then left the office.

William was resting on the couch in his living room when he received a call. He checked the ID and saw it was a number he did not recognize.

"Hello?"

"Good morning, am I speaking to Mr. William Washington?" a woman asked bluntly from the other end.

"Yes, this is he."

"I am calling you on behalf of the Federal Court to inform you of the dismissal of case 88 C 1777 due to lack of jurisdiction in Federal Court," she began to explain in a monotonous voice. "This means your scheduled hearing for June 16, 1999, will not hold tomorrow," she finished.

"What about the statute of limitations?" he inquired, still tense from the information he had just received.

"This means the statute of limitations for your case has been extended by one year," the woman replied dryly. William held the phone with his other palm and shouted into the room.

"Thank you very much for this information, ma'am," he replied, then hung up the phone. He screamed audibly a couple of times, prompting his children to ask if everything was all right.

"Everything's fine, sweeties! Nothing for you to worry about!" he shouted upstairs to reassure them he was still sane.

William began to feel more powerful and in control. He thanked God for answering his prayer in the courtroom and began feeling like he could win this case. Things were finally looking up. God had now given him a full year to prepare, gather more facts, and refile the case in the Illinois Circuit Court in Cook County.

William later found out his attorney, Mr. Harper, now knowing William had caught on to his shenanigans, filed a motion to remove himself from the case. The judge, however, said that was an irrelevant issue because the case had already been dismissed.

William began to feel even more empowered. He had meetings with different lawyers before eventually signing a deal with one of them.

This new attorney was a foxy one. He seemed so impressed by William's findings and investigation into the tainted blood samples that he attempted to hire him on his own payroll. He gave William an offer to investigate an asbestos case. If the case were settled or won in court, Will would receive a percentage of the winnings. William accepted his offer.

William decided to have his former attorney, Mr. Harper, investigated by the Illinois Attorney Registration and Disciplinary Commission (ARDC) for dismissing his real estate case without his knowledge or permission. However, Mr. Harper was able to convince the ARDC board that he had done it with Will's full knowledge and permission. After he was exonerated of all wrongdoing, William confronted him.

"William! How are you today?!" Mr. Harper said in a boisterous tone, obviously boasting from his victory that day.

"Congratulations, you lied and escaped," William retorted, a frown displayed on his face.

"Escaped what?" Harper feigned surprise. "I have no idea what you mean, sir!"

William smiled sarcastically. He was disgusted and bitter that Harper had gotten away with it.

"You can't run away from the law forever," William said, looking him straight in the eye before walking away.

A few minutes later, as he was entering his car, Bethany called.

"Hey, Beth."

"You're angry. What's wrong?"

"How would you even know that?"

"I'm your older sister. It's my job to know that," Bethany replied. "So, what's wrong?"

"You know my former lawyer? The crappy one?"

"Yeah, the one you said was a double agent or something," Bethany answered, before pausing for a moment. "Wait, wasn't he the awful man who settled your real estate case without telling you?"

Her voice was raised. *Now who was upset?* William thought.

"Yep, the one and only," William affirmed. "I tried to get him to pay for settling my case without my permission, but he got away with it."

He could hear her sigh on the other end.

"I'm sorry, Will," she consoled.

"Yeah, I'll be fine," Will assured. He knew she always worried about him, sometimes even when there was no need to. "In other news, I'm starting my investigation of doctors Boyer and Veracruz." He decided to change the subject.

"Will, even though I'm skeptical about all this, I trust you and will support you," Bethany began to say. "But please, be careful."

"I will," William reassured while nodding his head as if she were there with him. The two siblings exchanged goodbyes before hanging up.

In the following days, William used all of his available resources to have the doctors involved in his mother's treatment investigated. He knew, however, that he had to first establish that the blood was indeed tainted; otherwise, it would be incredibly hard for him to convince anyone of any wrongdoing by the doctors and the hospitals. He eventually received a voicemail from North Shore Hospital replying to his inquiries about Dr. Boyer:

Mr. Washington, this is Dr. Henry from the laboratory at North Shore Hospital, returning your call. I did as much investigating as I could. As I told you before, it doesn't look like we will be able to find out much. Great Source Blood Company and the New Hope Blood Service say there's no way to trace the donor of this particular unit because it happened so long ago and because of the tremendous volume of units affected. It's overwhelming. As I mentioned, if you have any questions about the medical situation, you need to talk to your mom's doctor, who I believe you told me was Dr. Boyer. I can give you his office number: 773-731----. I did give him your name and number the last time we spoke. I thought he was going to follow up with a phone call to you. I don't know if he has or not. But if you have any medical questions, that's who you need to be talking to. Thanks for your call back. See you later.

William groaned in dissatisfaction. It seemed they were not able to get anything from the looks of it. Whether that was due to interference from the higher-ups at the hospital or a cooperative cover-up in which everyone was involved remained a mystery to him. He didn't even get a reply on Veracruz, and his own investigations had not borne anything substantial. William still didn't give up. He continued to research medical records, court documents, and FDA documents, halfheartedly hoping that the Illinois Department of Public Health would conduct their query and investigation on the matter. William hoped something they found would be useful to him.

He kept on writing to the Illinois Department of Public Health and they kept giving him the same generic answer: it was under investigation. After a while, he came to realize that they were probably not looking into it as seriously as he had hoped. They said they would look into it as a grievous matter, but he didn't think they meant it. He decided to go to his lawyer to see what he could do.

"So, what do you think I should do?" William inquired after explaining all his issues and inability to find valuable evidence for his case. His attorney paused for a minute, furrowing his brows while thinking.

"You couldn't find anything on the doctors? At all?" the attorney asked to be sure. William shook his head in disappointment.

"And you still haven't heard anything substantial from the Illinois Department of Public Health, right?" he asked again. William made the same gesture.

"Then, honestly, we'll just have to go with what we have," he explained. "We can't keep waiting on them forever."

This reminded William that the deadline for filing was in just a few months.

"Oh, yes," he said, changing the subject. "What

about the filing of the case? The deadline would soon be up."

"Alright," the attorney assured, sitting up from his resting position. "I'll handle it."

William was surprised. Would he handle it?

"You will?" he asked, still surprised at the answer he received. "Okay then."

"You hired me, William," his lawyer noted. "Let me do my job. I'll handle it."

William was elated and thanked his lawyer before leaving his office. On his way to his car, he wondered how good his attorney was compared to the former one.

To his surprise, his attorney had still not filed the case, though the date for the statute of limitations crept up slowly but surely. William decided to meet with him at his office again.

"Hello, Mr. Washington," his attorney greeted. He offered William a seat, which William accepted.

"Good day," William started. "I came here to talk to you about the filing of the case."

"Mr. Washington, you hired me to be a lawyer, and that is what I am doing," the man said, with Will listening attentively. "I told you I would file it, and I will. There are things I have to do with regards to your case before filing it. You have to trust me that I will file it," he finished. This put William more at ease.

"Sorry," Will apologized. "I find it hard to trust you guys after what happened with my previous lawyer."

The problems Mr. Harper had caused him had put him ever on alert with his current attorney.

"I am not Mr. Harper," he assured Will. "And not only will I file this case, but we are also going to win."

William and his attorney discussed some other minor case details before he left the office. As the date neared, he reminded his lawyer one more time about the need to file the case before the statute of limitations was met, but he still did nothing. It was then that William concluded that the lawyer might have never intended to file the case, so William promptly fired him and terminated his services.

A month before the statute of limitations was up, William sat on his couch in the living room, drinking and in a down mood. He had no substantial evidence on the doctors, had not received a reply with anything helpful from the Illinois Department of Public Health and had no lawyer. His mind wandered to a lot of things but was mostly on his mother, who might be disappointed in him for not being able to make any leeway.

"I tried," he said to himself, but he was really talking to his mama. "I tried, Mama, but nothing is going well." His eyes were red, but he fought away the impending tears.

"I don't know if I can do this anymore, Mama," he kept saying. "It's like my life is on hold because of this case. I don't know what to do."

After letting his mind roam for an hour, he decided to try and contact the blood supplier. He was able to get in contact with the company's lawyer, who also happened to be the vice president.

"What do you want, Mr. Washington?"

"I...would like to settle," William said slowly.

The lawyer paused. He seemed unsure of what angle William was playing.

"So why isn't your lawyer calling me?" He asked cautiously.

"I fired my lawyer, and I am now representing myself," William replied in an attempt to reassure them this wasn't some ploy.

"Okay," the man said bluntly. "We will get back to you, Mr. Washington."

A few days later, William received a written offer of $10,000 to settle the case. He pondered on the offer for a while. He knew this case had already taken a lot of money out of him and accepting the deal would go a long way in recovering some of the money he had expended on the case. He also knew if he accepted this offer, no further legal action against any of the defendants would be possible, and they would get away with it. He would be letting his mother down, letting Spector down, and most of all, letting all the victims—past, present and future—down. He needed advice and decided to call the one person he trusted most.

"Hello, Will?"

"Hey, Beth."

"What's wrong this time?" she asked, and he

laughed. He went on to explain his current predicament and all the pros and cons of taking the offer from the blood suppliers.

"Well, all I can say is whatever you do, Mama isn't going to hold it against you," she assured. "She would know you tried. That's what matters. If you decide not to take it, that means you are going to keep trying. If you decide to take it, you have tried." She tried to encourage her younger brother, which was what he so desperately needed. "It has to be your choice," she said calmly.

"Thanks, Beth."

He had a difficult choice to make. He had to think about his family and his kids, but he also had to think about other people's families and kids. Take the deal or not?

CHAPTER EIGHT

'I cannot take the money.'

WILLIAM SAT AT his desk with the check in his hand, wondering what to do next. This was a crossroad he had no answer to but he wanted to make the right decision. Bethany was not helpful either. He stared at the check for the longest time, hoping that something, someone, would help him make this really tough decision.

On one hand, he was considering taking the money. He had spent so much time, effort, and finances bringing the case this far. Without a good enough lawyer to help him push this further and the statute of limitations coming up, it seemed more logical to take it.

On the other hand, he had come this far; too far, in fact, to give up. Collecting the money made him feel like a sell-out; it made him feel like the only thing he was after was the money, and that was not the case. He thought about the thousands of people affected by this problem. He thought again about his mother. *Maybe if*

I sleep over it, I'll be able to decide, he thought to himself. With that, he tucked the check in a folder and headed to bed.

That night, he slept and dreamed of nothing. When he had decided to sleep, he had hoped that his mother or Spector would appear and tell him what to do. But with no dreams and no appearance from Spector or his mother, he realized this was all his decision to make. Maybe Beth was right when she said their mother would understand no matter the decision he made at the end of the day.

As he got out of bed, his mind went straight to the television. He turned it on. The person on the screen had a white handkerchief in one hand and was dabbing at her face. For some reason, William was captivated by the scene. He found himself settling in to watch it, his curiosity towards why she was crying carrying more weight than any other thought on his mind. After about a minute of letting her cry, the presenter spoke in a soft tone.

"It must have been really tough for you to deal with people higher up than you trying to silence you," the presenter said."

The lady on the screen seemed much calmer after the suggestion, and when she spoke, her voice was steady.

"It was, indeed. It's one thing to know the truth and have the power to fight for it to come to life. It's another ball game entirely when you know the truth, want the whole world to know the truth, but you really don't have the power to spread that message. It's even worse when the people involved in this are much more powerful than you are, with big attorneys, big names, and lots of money to shut you up."

William sat up in his seat. This seemed like something that was of interest to him. He knew what it felt like to be in this woman's shoes because that was the same position he was in! It was just his luck that he went straight for the television this morning, something he never usually did. There was indeed a reason for everything in life, and now he was starting to believe it more.

"What made you decide to tell your truth in spite of the threats from these people? Because we just talked about the fact that they outright threatened you, they tried to buy you with money and other tempting offers, and they had lawyers to do all their work for them. What made you ignore all of this and choose to expose them?"

"Well, I think I really thought about it and decided it wasn't worth it, selling myself out, that is. I would never have been able to live with myself in the end. It would have made me much richer and maybe more successful to take the money, but at the end of the day, would my conscience be able to take it? Would I be able to spend that money without thinking of how the truth was suppressed because of it? A lot of people were affected by this man and his company, and they couldn't step forward with the truth because they were scared."

"I thought that this was the only way to help them; by speaking my truth. I thought that if I decided to speak out, maybe other people would decide to come out and speak their truths as well. The justice system seemed like it wasn't ready to fight for me, or perhaps, I didn't have enough power to make it fight for me. So, I decided to do this for them; for everyone who has no one to speak up for them. They had people in high places to fight their battles for them, people who could shut me up for food. I had only one thing working for me: my words. Why not use those words to speak my truth?"

"Was it hard finding someone to publish your article on the evil that happened?"

"Argh, yes, it was. It would have been easy to send it to a publishing house and have them publish it, but I guess they were scared of the same truth coming out about their own companies. These people were mostly in cahoots with their bosses and all, so it would be super easy to kill the story. I guess some people were scared of libel, too. So, they refused to publish. It was only logical to go independent with this story. Thankfully, I found someone who was ready to take a chance."

"So, you thought to publish your findings in the news?"

the man inquired.

"Everyone reads the news. They deserved to know the truth."

"Any last words for people out there who are or were in your shoes?"

William sat even straighter in his seat. Her message was why he was there all along.

"If you're in the same position as I was and you're wondering what to do, just do what is best for you. But remember that whatever decision you make affects a lot more people. It's your decision, but it's not just for you. It might seem like the hard thing to do but let your truth prevail."

"Alright, people..." the presenter started to say, but William wasn't paying attention anymore.

He was thinking about how all of this fit in the grand scheme of events. He had been moved to the television for a reason, and now he could see why. This was no ordinary coincidence. The TV program was about a lady who was oppressed by the powers that be; something very similar to what he was going through.

This was a sign. His mother and Spector might not have appeared to him in a dream, but this was them encouraging him! He could feel it in his bones that this was the push he was looking for.

William jumped out of his chair and grabbed his computer. He needed to find out who the woman on TV was and what she was fighting for. Maybe if he understood her struggles, he could relate them with his. As he grabbed his laptop, he felt a gentle breeze blow past him and he found himself relaxing slightly. Maybe this was another sign. He chose to see it as such.

He searched the internet for the name of the journalist, hoping to find her article or something related on the web. Immediately after he entered her name, the search results he found pushed him to look for more information.

The lady had been working as a pharmacist for one of the big pharmaceutical companies in the city. According to the report, she had found out that some of the drugs made by this company were doing more harm than good.

It was even worse when she found out the company was running human trials on people without adequately informing them of the things they were doing. As if that weren't enough, the company also didn't speak on the side effects and how bad things could get for those tested.

She had gone to her direct supervisor's boss to let him know, thinking it was just her supervisor trying to cut corners. She was shut down immediately and told to go with the flow. That was when she started doing her research. She quickly found out almost half of the current trials at the multinational company were equally duplicitous.

Seeing as this was beyond her, she threatened to expose them and sue them in court. That was when the threats started. She found out soon enough that they had high-up attorneys and even judges on their payroll.

They were also in bed with politicians. It was at this point that she found someone else in the company willing to go the extra mile with her and expose the company through the media.

When William finished reading her bio and the

actual article in which she exposed this company, he was confident that he had found this woman based on some divine intervention. He could see why he had been led there. The themes were the same.

From this, he learned that there was so much cover up in the medical field. For a big-time pharmaceutical company to stoop to the level of making outright threats to a former employee, it meant that there was so much more to the medical field than meets the eye. It also meant that he was quite lucky because no one had come to threaten his person. They had only managed to use their lawyers and the board to cover up their mess.

He extended his research a little further into the pharmaceutical industry and saw that there were other speculations about unapproved human trials. All they needed was someone to stand up and speak out against it.

He could see the impact her reporting was having. Families that were involved in the trials were slowly coming out to speak against the company and were asking for recompense.

Thinking about all of this made him feel that his decision was easier to make. He was no longer looking at it from his angle. The only angle he was looking at it from was that of the other people that might have been affected.

Perhaps if he made his own article, an exposé on the tainted blood incident, many more people would be able to understand what happened to their relatives and finally have the closure they sought.

This time, he didn't need to think about appearing before lawyers and judges or drawing out evidence that had long gone cold. He would present the facts and the people would make their conclusions based on their situations. He may even end up writing a book about his experiences. This time, he would make an actual difference and the world would hear of it. This decision may not have enriched his pockets, but he was sure that it would enrich his soul.

William Washington picked up his phone and made that one call he knew would change everything. He made a call to the blood supply company's vice president. The voice at the other end of the phone was surprised when he mentioned his decision.

"Hello, sir. My conscience cannot be bought,'"

William said to the man.

"I cannot take the money."

As he took out his laptop to put his thoughts and experiences into words, he felt a force squeeze his shoulder in that all too familiar, motherly grip. And then he felt another squeeze on his other shoulder. Deep down within him, William knew he couldn't have made a better decision than this.

CHAPTER NINE

Doctors indicted!

T HE AIR THAT wafted up to his nostrils that morning felt different. It felt cleaner. It seemed to cleanse his soul as he breathed in and out.

He had not felt this way in a long while; not since his mother passed on. Or rather, not since his mother was killed by the actions of others. But this morning, it felt different to live on earth.

If anyone had asked William how he felt at that moment, he would have told them that he felt like he owned the world.

He would explain to them that the feeling in his chest was similar to watching the end of a really good movie or coming to the last pages of an amazing, well-written book.

He would explain that it felt like sitting together with his entire family, enjoying his mother's home-cooked meal. That was how at-peace he felt.

But no one asked, so he kept his feelings and his joy to himself. You didn't have to ask him in order to know the way he felt, though.

It was evident in the smile deeply etched on his face, in the extra bounce in his strides as he walked; this was a man who finally achieved his goal.

William Washington read through the words on his laptop screen again and smiled to himself for the umpteenth time that morning. The words in the email were the reason behind it.

It had taken so long for him to get here. His heart was gladdened by the fact that someone finally believed in him and his story enough to want to publish it.

It had been hard at first, finding everything he needed to expose UBS, Dr. Boyer, and Dr. Veracruz, getting enough research material to work with, and then finally writing the article.

When he was finished writing the first draft of his article, he sent emails to over ten newspapers that he thought might help publish it. In the email, he explained a little about the story he wanted to share without giving them the entire thing, to prevent them from stealing the story from him.

He waited for over four weeks, yet none of them replied to him. He was starting to wonder if this was a wrong decision when finally; one of them asked him to send the story pitch. Swiftly, he researched what a pitch was and the template and then sent one to the man. In response, he received:

Dear Mr. Washington,

I was excited to get your pitch, and I think this is something we can work with.

I'm sorry about your mother's death, and I do hope that, with this article, we can make a difference and help other families like yours.

I'd be excited to work personally on this with you. If it wouldn't be too much trouble, would you like to meet for coffee? We can discuss your story better and how I can come in. I can make time for you by tomorrow if you'd like.

Do get back to me on your decision.

Regards,

Jonathan

William didn't need to think about it before he sent a reply to the man confirming that he would be available to meet with him the next day. Keeping it close to his chest, William set out of the house the next day without telling anyone what he planned to do. There was no use getting anyone's hopes up without being certain of the situation himself.

The minute he saw Jonathan, he was again reassured that this was a good decision. The tell-tale wary feeling he got with the lawyers wasn't there when he walked up to the man, and throughout their meeting, it didn't come up at all. William had finally found someone who would help him fight the long fight.

Again, he explained to Jonathan everything that

had happened from the very first moment until the point they were sitting together. William felt different explaining things to this man. He didn't blindly nod when William spoke; it felt like he was really listening to William. When William finished, Jonathan took a sip of his coffee, pausing for a minute before he finally spoke.

"I'm sorry about everything you've been through," Jonathan said.

"I was really touched when I read your article, and I felt it was something we have to be a part of. We are very keen about the truth and outing wrong with our newspaper."

"Thank you for agreeing to do this for me," William nodded.

"It's nothing. I'll personally take this up. This piece is going to be my baby until we publish. I will work on it like it is my very own story," Jonathan reassured.

"I'd really appreciate that, Jonathan. Is there any way that any of the people responsible for my mother's death can be held accountable?"

"Well, it's been so long. For the case against the hospital, the statute of limitations has passed, as you know. But here's what we can do with your article. We can make it such that those who were involved, the doctors who made these decisions and covered them up, can be made to pay for their mistakes,"

Jonathan looked William square in the eyes.

William sat up in his chair and drew closer to Jonathan.

"How's that?"

"It's simple enough, yet slightly tricky. All we have to do is pitch one party against the other. The hospital might not have had a direct hand in your mother's death, but from what you say, the doctors were aware that something was very wrong after her transfusions. It was only logical for them to tell you these things in the beginning. They covered it up until it got out of hand without telling you."

"What we'd do is to pit the hospital against the doctors. Make it clear in the article that we're certain the hospital and the medical body would never condone such indiscipline. We hint at them needing to take action."

"And then we make the people fall on your side by awakening their emotional response. In all of this, we keep hammering the fact that these two doctors did you a disservice. I'm pretty sure, in a bid not to look bad to society, the hospital and medical board would make a move. When it comes to your ass and another person's, no right-minded individual will cover someone else's over their own,"

Jonathan finished.

"You think this will work?"

William asked, a part of him getting scared already.

"We don't have many options. We can only try and keep our fingers crossed."

And try, they did.

THE DAY WILLIAM got the good news he was in his home, weeks after his first meeting with Jonathan.

"William!"

Bethany shouted from the door as she knocked. He could hear the excitement in his sister's voice even though she was still far away.

That excitement was enough of a reward for all the trouble he had been through the few past years.

As he walked to the door, William found himself reminiscing about the things that had happened in the last few weeks.

After meeting with Jonathan, he had gone back to the drawing board and gathered as many facts as he could on the case. He had written the article again, as Jonathan suggested, putting Drs Boyer and Veracruz in the spotlight.

After writing the article, he went back to Jonathan for another edit. A few back and forth cycles later, the final draft for the piece was done, and it was everything William hoped it would be. The very next day, the article was published.

William could still smell his fear as Jonathan told him they were running the story the next day. He was worried about how people would receive the news.

That, coupled with the fact that Jonathan could not assure him it would make the cover page, scared him. The front page was usually for more recent and often controversial stories that would sell the newspaper.

He had been shocked when the piece came out, and it had a byline on the cover page. Jonathan, who wanted to surprise him, had not told him until he got a copy of the newspaper himself! The rest had fallen into place.

The outcry of the readers was unexpected. People reacted to the piece in ways that surprised William. Much to his surprise, the very next day, other newspapers started to talk about the tainted blood incident of the 90s again. Soon enough, he was getting calls asking him if they could feature some parts of his story in their papers.

The week that followed was even crazier. It wasn't only in print. Television and radio stations were talking about the tainted blood incident and the number of lives that were affected. It stopped being just about William's story; it was about the others as well.

The backlash on the hospitals and medical boards was immense. Jonathan had been right! All it took was turning them against each other. In a bid to look good, the boards had come out to say that they would look into the matter and investigate the doctors. William was almost sure that would never happen, but then, they really did start to investigate the doctors.

All of this had taken weeks. William had been fighting this battle for years unsuccessfully. It had taken his words, a supportive structure in Jonathan, and all the willpower he could ever have. William was more than grateful to Spector. If it hadn't been for Spector, he never would have thought to publish his story in the newspaper.

William got to the door just as this thought crossed his mind. He opened the door to see his sister beaming with joy, yet tears slid down her face.

"It is finally happening, William!"

she cried as she walked in.

"It has happened!"

"Calm down, Beth. What's happening?"

"Mama is finally getting the justice she deserves," she cried, tossing the newspaper in her hands at her brother.

Doctors Indicted in Tainted Blood Cover-up, the headline read. A quick scan of the article and he found the two names he had memorized after years of trying; Boyer and Veracruz. William's eyes misted with tears. It was indeed finally happening.

"They've been indicted for covering up and hiding the things they did!"

William cried.

"Your article started a huge chain of events. It was only a matter of time before other people with suspicions also started coming out. The board already has them suspended, from what I hear."

William reached for the nearest chair and sank into it. For all the years he had been fighting this, he had never thought of how he'd feel or what he'd do if it succeeded.

He felt drained and excited all at once. His body was a mix of emotions he couldn't name. Bethany knelt before him and cradled his face in her hands.

"You did it, Will! You finally did it! I'm so sorry I didn't stand by you as I should have. I just didn't know how…"

Beth congratulated her brother.

William held his sister's hand and shushed her in the gentlest tone he could muster.

"You shouldn't speak like that. You supported me in your own way. You couldn't have known."

"But you did. You knew. I should have, too,"

she wept.

"Oh, sister mine, I had help,"

he whispered.

"Today, Bethany, is not the day to regret or feel sad. It is the day to rejoice, dear sister."

"Yes! I'll get some wine. We should be celebrating,"

Bethany replied.

As she rose to her feet and headed towards the kitchen, William found himself looking at the paper again. All he could think of was that if it hadn't been for Spector, this would not have happened. If it hadn't been for him, he probably would never have seen the program about the lady who ousted the pharmaceutical company using a news story. In a way, it had been Spector's doing.

"Thank you,"

he whispered into the air as he rose to join his sister.

He could almost swear that he heard Spector say, *'You're welcome.'*

EPILOGUE

WILLIAM WASHINGTON SAT in his living room feeling like something was missing. He couldn't shake the feeling that deep down within him there was something that needed filling; an incomplete mission. The feeling had been with him since his news article had made such an uproar the past few months.

One would think that with the rate at which the story had become popular, he would have felt fulfilled. But something still felt a little off, and he could not place his finger on it.

He could feel Spector's presence around him as he settled in to enjoy his morning coffee. Spector had started to be more present in his life of late.

Now that he was retired and often home alone, he believed Spector sensed his need for companionship and was sticking by him. He had given William the encouragement and direction he needed to get the story out. Maybe he was telling him something again.

When he was done with his coffee, he headed out to the front porch to pick up the day's paper. Stepping out the door, he felt the warm morning sun on his face and a calming breeze blowing on him. He suddenly felt the need to take a short stroll. Tucking the paper under his armpit, he started to walk.

While he was out, William thought about what he had been through as he tried to get justice for himself and his family. It had been a tough time, but things were shaping up. He remembered his first lawyer, Mr. Harper.

A smile crept upon his face as he remembered what he did to him when he worked as his real estate attorney. He remembered how he hadn't even done a good enough job on his mother's case, either.

It excited him to know that he was now smiling when he thought of him. Back then, he was always bitter and angry when he remembered his name. He had done William a lot of wrongs. William had even gotten Mr. Harper investigated by the Illinois Attorney Registration and Disciplinary Commission (ARDC) for dismissing his real estate case without permission.

William just wanted to get justice for the wrongs Mr. Harper caused him. Mr. Harper had gotten away with his wrongdoing back then because he was able to convince the ARDC he had dismissed William's case with his full knowledge.

It crossed his mind that he should find out about Mr. Harper. While he was surprised this thought crossed his mind, he was determined to do just that; find out about him. He decided to call his brother-in-law because he felt like a lawyer might know how to find Mr. Harper. He walked back home feeling lighter and better than he'd felt when he left for his walk.

As soon as William arrived home, he dialed Tony's phone number and told him what he had been thinking about.

"Mr. Harper? You don't know what happened to him?"

Tony asked.

"Something happened to him? What?"

William asked.

"He got disbarred some time ago. He had gone ahead to settle a case without consulting his client first, almost like what he did with you. And like that was not bad enough, he collected some money from the opposing guys. It was a big mess at the time. I thought you knew,"

Tony explained.

"Nah, man. I had no idea. I'm pretty shocked right now,"

William replied.

"Well, prepare for an even bigger shocker. I tried calling you earlier, but you didn't answer."

Tony changed the subject.

"I was out walking. What's the matter?"

William asked.

"Remember the guys who came to the house and attacked you and Beth a long time back? The one that shot you?"

"Yeah?"

William replied, wondering where this discussion was headed.

"He's finally been caught."

"What?"

William asked in surprise. "For shooting me?"

"Not initially. He was arrested for another crime entirely. The sketch they made when Beth described him back then was somehow pulled out, and now, they're going to charge him for your shooting as well. He's got a long time to rot in jail."

William sighed deeply. This was an unexpected turn of events for him. First, Mr. Harper, and now the shooter would pay for his crimes as well. It was as though all of the people that were part of the injustices back then were paying for their sins, one after another.

He had even learned from a local newspaper article that a tragic auto accident had struck one of the doctor's family members. It didn't end there, however. One of the hospitals that was involved in this case had even closed down. It was like Karma had decided to strike and bring justice to whom it was due.

William said his goodbyes to his brother-in-law with a promise to be in touch with him soon. He turned to the newspaper he'd fetched earlier and started to read through. The front page of the newspaper shocked him more than anything else that morning.

Governor Willis, the state governor at the time the tainted blood incident happened, was plastered all over the front page. According to the report, the governor had been implicated in a corruption case involving the misappropriation of funds when he was in government. It was so bad, and the evidence was so glaring, that it wouldn't bode well for the governor. There was also a video recording implicating the governor.

The unsatisfied feeling he'd had that morning momentarily dissipated. It was as though all the news he'd heard today was what his soul had been waiting for to feel complete fulfillment. Justice was indeed served. It had taken a long time, and it was not in the manner he thought it would be, but justice was served. William could rest easier now.

He walked to his computer to read more on the governor's indictment. He had a keen interest in this case and he wanted to follow it through. Turning on his computer, he first opened his email, a habit he had gotten so used to over time that it had become a part of him. He decided to read his emails since the page was loading already.

When William opened his first email, he stared at the message in disbelief. Today was indeed the best day of his life. Staring back at him was an email from a publicist offering him money for the rights to his story. The publicist was looking to do a book and make a movie. He was offering William ten million dollars as a starting offer.

William was shocked by the amount. He could never have imagined this would happen. He remembered his mother's prayer when he was shot. She had prayed for him to be a beacon of hope and save many lives. He had done just that with his news articles and here God was rewarding him for choosing truth over the ten thousand dollars he had been offered. God had repaid him in multiple folds.

William smiled as he typed his reply. Of course, he would take the offer. Today was the first day of the rest of an amazing life.

BIOGRAPHY

ELVIS IS THE author of eight books and many published articles. He has taught criminal justice at the college level as a part-time criminal justice instructor. Elvis is married with three adult children. His oldest daughter and son in-law are dentists. His younger daughter holds a Master's in Public Administration and specializes in fundraising and project management. His son is a graduate of Purdue University, specializing in IT.

OTHER BOOKS BY ELVIS SLAUGHTER

Mentally Ill Inmates and Corrections – Coming Soon
Preschool to Prison
Safer Jail and Prison Matters
The American Genocide
The Ghosts of Hollandale
Uncle Percy's Blessings
The Malcolm X Project
Epiphany Or Sin
Egomaniac

Available at Amazon.com **and**
www.elvisslaughter.com